HER PASSIONATE **HERO**
A BLACK DAWN NOVEL
BOOK 3

CAITLYN O'LEARY

© Copyright 2018 Caitlyn O'Leary
All rights reserved.
All cover art and logo © Copyright 2018
By Passionately Kind Publishing Inc.
Cover by Lori Jackson Design
Editing by Sandy Ebel - Personal Touch Editing

All rights reserved. No part of this book may be reproduced in any form or by any electronic or mechanical means, including information storage and retrieval systems—except in the case of brief quotations embodied in critical articles or reviews—without permission in writing from the author.

This book is a work of fiction. The names, characters, and places portrayed in this book are entirely products of the author's imagination or used fictitiously. Any resemblance to actual events, locales or persons, living or dead, is entirely coincidental and not intended by the author.

The unauthorized reproduction or distribution of this copyrighted work is illegal. Criminal copyright infringement, including infringement without monetary gain, is investigated by the FBI and is punishable by up to five years in federal prison and a fine of $250,000.

If you find any eBooks being sold or shared illegally, please contact the author at Caitlyn@CaitlynOLeary.com.

DEDICATION

Dedicated to those who are serving and who have served.

SYNOPSIS

Sometimes the harder you fall, the stronger you rise.

As the Vice Principal of one of the toughest of schools in East L.A., Aliana Novak knows what it's like to be bullied, but until he graduated, she had her own personal protector, Hunter Diaz. The following two years were filled with horrific experiences that molded her into the woman she is today. Now she is standing up for the right thing, a gang is threatening her life.

Hunter Diaz scraped and fought his way out of the gangs of East L.A. to serve honorably as a SEAL in the United States Navy. He has become one of the most dangerous men on the planet. When he finds out Aliana is threatened by gangs, he returns to the place he vowed to leave firmly in the past.

Hunter expects to find the same awkward and fragile girl he once knew. Instead, he finds a beautiful, strong woman who is closed off from everything but the children under her care. Even when her life is on the line, she is determined to handle things on her own. Can Hunter prove to Aliana that she is not in this fight alone before she ends up dead?

CHAPTER ONE

"He's ours. You interfere one more time, and I will gut you, bitch."

Sweat trickled down Aliana's back, as blood trickled down her neck. Her arms ached from being held from behind. Whoever had her, must've wanted to dislocate her shoulders.

"Tell me you understand."

"Yes," she said in Spanish. "I understand."

The knife dug in deeper. More blood gushed. She knew Mateo, he wasn't going to kill her. She'd known him for six years. She'd taught him how to write an essay. Okay, maybe she had only gotten through how to write a strong opening sentence, but still, she'd gotten through. He wouldn't kill her. Hurt her, yes, kill her no.

"Stop filling his head with worthless dreams."

"They're not worthless. Your brother has potential. He can get a scholarship and go to college."

"Goddamn right, he has potential. He has potential right where he is, with *Los Demonios*. That's where he needs to stay."

The knife was sharp and hurt as it slid downward along the skin of her throat. She needed to be quiet. Maybe he *would* kill her.

"Let us play with her first. Please, Mattie. She's got great tits," a weasel-faced teenager said from beside Mateo.

The man behind her jerked her arms harder, thrusting her breasts into prominence.

"I want to fuck her before you kill her," weasel boy continued.

Her sweat turned to icicles.

"Back off, Berto." She recognized the voice, but she couldn't see the face of the gang member. At least he wasn't suggesting she be raped.

Please God, say someone was monitoring the security cameras for once and had called the police. But then Aliana shut her eyes, remembering that her townhome's parking lot cameras had all been vandalized two days ago, and they hadn't had time to repair them. Was it possible Mateo had planned it?

"Both of you shut up, this is between me and the bitch," Mateo said.

She looked at the three males who surrounded her and thought about the male behind her who was intent on breaking her arms. They were still teenagers, okay, maybe Mateo was twenty or twenty-one now, but she needed to think of him as a teenager. The only way she could cope mentally was to think of them as boys. She couldn't think of them as men, she had to pretend they were her students.

"Mateo," she said crisply, using her Vice Principal voice. "This doesn't have to go any further. I know you're doing this for your family. I won't tell anybody about this incident if you'll leave now."

"You listen to me, whore. You convince my little brother he's better off with his posse."

Never. Never. Never.

The words were on the tip of her tongue.

"Be smart." She zeroed in on the voice and finally made out the face. Rafael Lopez. He'd hardly said a word in her class, but when he did, it was on point. Like now. She kept her mouth shut.

"You gonna do what I tell you? You gonna stop giving my baby brother ideas?" How could these two be related? They didn't look alike, and they had nothing in common, it was like they were two different species.

"Answer me. You gonna do what I say?" Mateo asked again, his voice soft and deadly, his foul breath blowing in her face.

Now that the knife was gone, she could nod.

"Goddamn right, you won't, not unless you want your Mama carved up into itty bitty little pieces."

Aliana's head jerked, the knife dug in deep, before Mateo pulled the blade away from her neck.

"You stupid bitch, I'm not ready to kill you, yet. What are you doing?"

Her whole body started to tremble. "What do you know about my mother?" she demanded. She tried to keep her voice firm, but it came out weak.

"We've been following you. Your Mama is in that fancy old folk's home up in Glendale. Pretty stupid getting her a room on the first floor. I guess it's because it has that tree she can look at, huh? You know, anybody could sneak in. Who knows what could happen to her."

"You leave my mother alone." She was scared, her Czech accent thick. Aliana wondered if they would understand her. Nicolas was one thing, but her mother? Her mother was totally defenseless.

"I'm not sure you're going to remember this lesson." He brought the knife back up to the top of her blouse.

Snip. She watched as the second bounced onto the asphalt.

Snip. The third button bared her pink lacy bra and gold medallion.

"Pretty. I like lace."

She said nothing.

Mateo slid the knife underneath the delicate material of her bra. Aliana showed no emotion. She felt herself slipping away. She tried to stay in the moment. It was her only chance. She needed to defend herself, not slip away into nothingness. She struggled again, kicking out like she had when they'd first jumped her. The guy behind her just tightened his hold.

"Is that a siren?" That was Rafael's voice.

She cried out in pain when Mateo yanked the knife away. It ended up slicing into her chest while cutting her bra and chain.

"We're outta here." He waved the bloody knife in front of her face. "You remember what I said, bitch. You stop filling my brother's head with stupid fucking dreams. If you mention anything to the cops, your mother will get the full treatment before we kill her, it doesn't matter how old she is, a slut is a slut, you get my meaning? Then we start cutting her."

Aliana thought of her invalid mother suffering the worst fate imagineable and started to moan.

The guy behind her shoved her, and she slammed into her little hybrid. She caught a glimpse of his bald head as he and the others ran to their late model, silver muscle car and sped out of the parking lot. She scrambled for her purse and keys she had dropped when Mateo had spun her around. She took precious extra seconds to find the St. Rita medal and put it in her purse, not caring if the chain was lost. As soon as she found everything, she hit the release button and practically fell into her car.

On instinct, she started the engine. For a second, she thought about the groceries that littered the pavement, then she let out a harsh laugh. She considered getting out of her car to go inside her townhome, but that didn't feel safe. Neither did staying in her car and calling the police. She needed to leave.

She had trouble getting the car in reverse. She could barely see when she looked into the rearview mirror, it was like it was raining outside because of her tears. She swiped at her eyes. Better. *Get it together Novak.* She felt the air conditioning blast on her bare breasts and screeched to a halt in the townhome parking lot. Reaching into the backseat of her car hurt her arm, and she groaned as she grabbed her trench coat.

"Sakra!" She swore in Czech. She realized she hadn't put on her seatbelt as she struggled to put her coat on. Finally, she just put the coat on backward. It was the best she could do without getting out of the car. Aliana jammed on her seatbelt, wiped her eyes with the sleeve of her jacket, and pulled out of her complex.

She had to get away. She didn't know where. She couldn't go to the police. Where was she going to go? Where? Finally she figured it out. She had to get to her mother.

"Bastard," she yelled. He almost hit her. It was then she realized she had just run a red light. *"Sakra!"* she swore again in Czech. Tears started to fall in earnest. She could barely see out the window. She had to pull over. Then she saw red and blue lights behind her. She pulled into a gas station and parked near the air pump. Nobody was there. She shuddered when she saw a big shadow outside her window. She jumped when the loud knock sounded beside her.

"Ma'am?"

She couldn't stop crying. She tried. But she couldn't.

"Ma'am, are you all right?"

A bright light shined into the car, she couldn't see anything. Aliana rested her head against her steering wheel. Why did she hurt? Why were her hands slippery?

"Ma'am, open the door."

Aliana jerked her head to the door, taking solace the door was locked.

"Ma'am, I'm a police officer. Look at my uniform." The light was gone, and she saw it was now shining on the man who was talking. He was older than Mateo and his friends, and he was wearing a police uniform. He looked worried.

"Can you roll down your window?"

It took a moment for Aliana to understand what he was asking. Police. He was a policeman. Oh God, not the police. He knocked on the window again. She had to respond. She pressed the button that rolled down the window.

"Why are you bleeding?" he asked quietly. "Did someone hurt you?"

She gulped. She tried to say something, but the words stuck. She put her hands to her throat. They came away wet. She extended her blood-soaked hand out the window, showing the officer as the blood slowly dripped off the tips of her fingers. It took a moment for her to stop staring at the beautiful red of the blood and see that he was talking into his shoulder. He said something about an ambulance.

"You're going to be okay." He reached into the car through the window and unlocked the door. Aliana heard a whimper. Oh God, it had actually come from her. Her tears burned the cut on her throat, and she tried to stop them from dripping off her chin.

"I'm going to open the door, okay?"

What was he saying? She felt more of the hot night air hit her as it rushed in the door. Bewildered, she looked up into warm brown eyes. For a moment, she thought she was seeing a ghost from the past. She shook her head to clear it, and the features of the policeman became clear.

"Are you cut anywhere else besides your throat?"

She had to think. Eventually, she nodded.

"May I see?"

She shook her head wildly. "It's not bad." Her teeth chattered. She didn't want to take off her coat and show her breasts.

"Can you tell me what happened?"

She opened her mouth to tell him about Mateo. "Ahhh." Was all that came out. She thought about her mother in her first floor room at the nursing home. How had he known she had a small little place in Glendale? He even knew about the Jacaranda tree. More tears spilled.

"Miss? Can you tell me what happened?"

She heard a siren. Not some figment of her imagination.

"Who did this to you?"

She shook her head.

He sighed. "Can you tell me your name?"

She coughed and covered her throat. "Aliana Novak," she whispered.

A woman in a blue shirt was suddenly beside the police officer. "I need to see my patient," she said. The policeman moved. She crouched down in front of Aliana. "Can you get out of the car?" she asked gently.

Aliana considered her question, then nodded. She shouldn't have, it hurt. More tears fell. Why couldn't she stop crying? She needed to suck it up. She wasn't a crier. She hadn't cried in years. This wasn't who she was. The tears stopped. There. She was back to being Aliana Mila Novak. She saw the woman give her an odd look, but then she smiled.

"Are you injured under your coat?"

"He cut off my blouse," Aliana said. The woman assisted her out of her car. "I'm bleeding on my chest. It hurts too."

"Can you walk?" she asked.

It was a stupid question. "Of course, I can walk." Aliana legs went out from under her as she got out of the car. When the officer and EMT grabbed an arm on either side to keep her from falling, she yelped in pain.

"What's wrong?" the woman asked.

"My arms hurt. One of them shoved them behind my back."

"Okay, we'll get you checked out."

They helped her over to the ambulance and got her inside.

"I'm going to shut the door so we can take off the coat and see your injury, is that okay?"

This time Aliana knew better than to nod. "Yes." Then she saw the other technician in the ambulance who was crouched down, getting something from a kit. "No," Aliana said as the woman started to help her out of her coat.

She looked over her shoulder. "Jerry, why don't you go outside and wait with the cop. I've got this."

"Sure thing."

After he left, Aliana cringed. "That was stupid. I'm sorry," Aliana said quietly, looking at the grimy floor of the ambulance.

"No, it wasn't," the technician assured her. "I wouldn't want to take off my shoes in front of Jerry," she said with a laugh. Aliana looked up into her sparkling green eyes. "How about we take you out of this? You must be sweltering."

She was. Aliana took a quick glance at the woman's name tag, it said Ritter. "Thank you for your help, Ms. Ritter."

"Call me Mary," the woman said as she tugged on the right sleeve of Aliana's coat. Aliana let out a cry, the lining of the coat had stuck to the wound. Mary immediately realized what was going on. "I'm going to cut this off." She turned to the same kit Jerry had been rooting around in. Aliana swiftly pulled off her coat, not letting out a sound now that she knew what to expect. When Mary turned around holding the scissors, she found her sitting on the gurney with her blouse open and the ugly cut seeping blood.

"You really shouldn't have done that," she said quietly.

"It was expedient."

"Okay. Let's take a look, shall we?"

Aliana wondered why she was saying we. Mary made a tsking sound. "I think there are a couple of spots here that are going to need stitches. We're going to take you to the hospital. When was the last time you had a tetanus shot?"

"I don't know." Aliana coughed and it hurt.

"Let's get you covered up." Mary gently helped Aliana into her coat, the right way. "I'm just going to tie the sash loosely, is that okay?"

Aliana nodded.

"Jerry's going to drive us. Ernie will follow us, he's going to want to get a statement."

At the mention of the policeman, Aliana's thoughts flew to her mom and how she'd looked last weekend. She'd tried to tidy up her thin hair, but even using the soft brush, her mother had cried and said it had hurt. For the last two months, Danica Novak had spent a lot of time whimpering like a small child. When Aliana had talked to the staff at the nursing home, they had assured her this was just a phase and there was no medical reason she would be in pain. Still, it broke her heart to hear her mother's soft sobs. It even happened when she rubbed the soothing vanilla lotion on her feet and hands.

Aliana would have insisted they bring in specialists if it weren't for the fact her mother would suddenly stop crying and start smiling and then thank her for the wonderful foot rub. It made Aliana's heartache, she never knew what she was going to encounter when she visited. The idea that Mateo was threatening her helpless mother both enraged and scared the hell out of her. There was no way she was going to tell the police even if that had been her original intention.

"Are you listening to me?"

"Hmmmm?" It was the same way she responded to students when she was multitasking and hadn't been listening to what they'd been saying.

"I said we're leaving for the hospital now. Ernie, the cop, is getting your belongings and locking up your car. He'll follow us to the hospital. He'll take your statement there."

"I ran a red light. He must be upset with me."

"It's okay." Mary patted her hand. "You're entitled. I want you to lie down. I need to get you strapped in, okay?"

Mary indicated the pillow, and Aliana shook her head. That was a mistake, she grabbed at her gauze covered neck. "Isn't there a place for me to sit? I don't want to lie down."

"Honey, I took your blood pressure. You're light headed. This is for the best."

"Please?"

"It's policy. You'd really be helping me out if you would just rest. It isn't far." Mary's eyes were soft and coaxing. Aliana stretched out on the gurney, and Mary did up the straps. "Thank you."

Aliana shut her eyes. Mateo's face swam in front of her closed lids. She slammed them back open and stared at the ceiling of the ambulance. She felt nauseous. She swallowed and bit back a groan of pain. Seriously, she needed to quit being a drama queen, this was nothing. Eventually, she felt the vehicle come to a stop. The rear doors opened, and the steamy heat of the night billowed into the back of the ambulance. It felt suffocating.

The straps wouldn't come off. She tried to get them off. The more she struggled and moved the more pain shot through her chest.

"Calm down, Miss, let me help." Jerry jumped into the back of the ambulance and loomed over her. Aliana shrieked.

"Jerry, move your ass. Let me," Mary said sharply.

"Sorry, sorry, sorry, sorry, sorry," Aliana repeated over and over again.

"You have nothing to be sorry for. Jerry is a dumbass. Let me get you unstrapped, and you can walk out, will that be okay with you?"

Aliana was free, she pushed up with Mary's help.

"Take it slow." She looked around. Jerry was standing outside looking contrite. She gave him a tentative smile, and he saluted. Mary put her arm around her waist. "Watch your step, it's a big one. Will you let Jerry help you?"

"Of course. I'm sorry for being out of control, I don't know what came over me." She held her hand out to him like a lady be handed out of a carriage. He took it like a courtier with a slight bow. Aliana gave a small grin in return.

There was an orderly waiting with a wheelchair. "Your chariot awaits," Jerry said.

"Now you've got it," Mary laughed.

"Thank you, both," Aliana said.

"It's our job," Jerry said. "Good luck."

The big orderly whisked her in through the double doors.

* * *

"Officer Robinson, it was dark. I can't describe them."

Aliana willed herself to treat this like she was in control, that she was having a conversation with the principal at her school. She could do this. She refused to give up her power again tonight. When she felt her hands begin to clench, she forced them to spread out and rest on her thighs.

"Can you walk me through it again? I still don't understand how you got away from them." She looked into his intelligent face. It was obvious he didn't believe her, and who could blame him. Her story sounded as flimsy as a piece of paper. From dealing with so many students, the one thing she knew is the kids who stayed closest to the truth, they were the ones who tended to get away with their crimes.

"I told you, one of the teenagers said he heard a siren."

"If you can't describe them, how do you know they are teenagers?"

That was a great question. How could she? "I deal with teenagers all the time at my school, there was just something about them that seemed like my students. I can't exactly explain it, but it was a sense I got it."

"Fifteen? Sixteen? Nineteen? What age did you *sense* them to be?" She looked down at the bed she was sitting on. At least she wasn't hurting, it was a good thing she hadn't allowed them to give her anything stronger than the local anesthesia, otherwise she wouldn't be sharp enough to navigate this interview.

"I'm not sure."

"Surely if you work with teenagers day in and day out, you can take a pretty accurate guess," he insisted.

Aliana tried to think of an excuse. "It was dark, and I was scared for my life, I'm sorry I wasn't paying better attention."

"Usually victims remember something," he said mildly.

She had to stick to her story. Her mother's life depended on it. They stared at one another. She knew his game. She played it often enough herself. She waited. And waited. And waited.

He blew out a breath. "If you can't tell me their ages. Can you tell me what they sounded like? Did you have an idea if they were African American? Hispanic? White?"

"Hispanic. They spoke Spanish. They drove away in a late model, hyped-up car."

"Well, at least that's something. Would you recognize the car if I showed you some pictures?"

She nodded. That shouldn't be giving too much away. The bandage scratched. When would she remember to stop doing that? How was she going to explain her injury when she got to school? A nasty kitchen accident wouldn't be believed, she thought wryly. Good, at least she found a little bit of humor. She was coping.

"Is something funny?" Officer Robinson asked sharply.

"I was thinking of excuses to explain my injury to the people at school," Aliana admitted. "Some of the stories were somewhat unbelievable."

"Imagine that." He sounded amused.

"Are we done?" she asked.

"I'm going to ask that you come to our station to look at pictures of cars. Can you make it tomorrow?"

"Yes." She needed to get to her mother. She looked down at the slim watch on her wrist and was thankful to see it was still only seven o'clock. Visiting hours lasted until nine o'clock, so she could still make it to Glendale if she could get a lift to her car.

"Yes?" The officer prompted.

"Can you take me to my car?"

"I intended to."

"Oh."

"You didn't think I was just going to leave you stranded, did you?"

"Well, yes."

He gave her an odd look. "They probably won't let you out of here for another hour."

"I can't afford to wait that long. I have somewhere to be." She started to hop off the bed, and Officer Robinson was immediately at her side helping her.

"You're an independent thing, aren't you?"

"I don't know what you're talking about." Aliana spied her purse on a chair in the corner of the room and grabbed it. "Do you know who I need to talk to get released? I already provided my insurance card."

"I would assume the doctor who treated you."

Aliana pulled the curtain open and glanced into the room for her doctor. "Hello," she called out when she spotted the man. "I need to leave. Can I go now?" He looked up from a chart he was reading. He looked harried. A nurse came up to talk to him at the same time somebody else yelled his name. He started to walk away without answering Aliana's question.

"Doctor. May I leave?" Aliana repeated more loudly.

He looked over his shoulder. "Yes. Go talk to the nurse at the front desk." Thank God for overcrowded hospitals.

She winced when she tied the sash tighter on her coat.

"Let me help." Officer Robinson knotted her coat so that it didn't bind as much. "I hope you're planning on going home."

"I told you, I have somewhere to be."

"Don't you need to change your clothes?"

Aliana dipped her chin to check the front of her coat, she saw the blood that stained the front. *Sakra.* Maybe they wouldn't notice at the nursing home. She *had* to get there.

"This is not really your concern."

She watched as he pulled out his phone. "Hi, this is Ernie. I'm taking a long lunch. I'll call you when I'm back on duty."

Why did he do that? "Does this mean you can't take me to my car?"

"This means I'm going to take you to your appointment, then I'm taking you to your car, then I'm following to your house and making sure you get in safely."

"Townhome."

"What?"

"I live in a townhome," she explained.

"Whatever. You need a keeper, and right now, I'm it."

He was mistaken. Very mistaken. The last thing she needed was someone to take care of her. She'd learned a long time ago there was nobody she could trust, and this man wasn't going to change her mind.

CHAPTER TWO

"Mama, how are you tonight?" Aliana asked in Czech. She looked down at the shrunken figure in the bed, hoping against hope tonight might be one of the nights that her mother recognized her. She just laid there, seemingly frozen in her own world. Aliana picked up her hand and gently rubbed in some of the vanilla scented lotion. "Doesn't that smell good?" she asked. Maybe she should have chosen the tube of rose scented lotion her mom liked. She'd used that scent exclusively when Aliana was growing up, but to this day Aliana gagged whenever she smelled it. It brought back too many bad memories. Nope, vanilla was the way to go.

"How's Mizz Dee doing tonight?" Shorinda asked as she came into the room.

"Quiet. Can't get a word out of her."

"How's Mizz A doing then?" Shorinda came closer to the bed. As soon as she did, she got a good look at Aliana and let out a screech. "What in the hell happened to you? My God, girlfriend, you're tore up."

"I was in a car accident," Aliana said.

"You're doing a shitty job of lying. You want to be believed, keep your eyes on me. Now, tell me the damned truth."

Aliana kissed her mom's hand and put it back under the thin blanket. "One of my former students got out of hand. He's pissed I'm trying to lead his baby brother into a better life. He threatened *Maminka* if I didn't stop trying to teach his brother." Aliana bit her lip so hard, the coppery flavor of blood burst into her mouth. "I've got to go talk to your administration about moving *Maminka* to a different room. They knew she was on the bottom floor with the Jacaranda tree in front of her window. If they move her, they have to leave this room empty."

"They're going to kick her butt out, Honey. There's not a chance in hell they're going to want this kind of trouble lurking around."

A quick flash of a guitar pick crossed her mind, and she forced it away. "I guess I knew that. It'll take me a day or two to figure out what to do." More than that if she was going to be honest with herself. It had taken her over a month to find such a good facility in the first place.

"Can I make a suggestion?" Shorinda asked.

"You're going to whether I agree or not, aren't you?" Aliana laughed wryly.

"I like that you're smart," Shorinda grinned. "I bet your mama was smart in her day. Here's my suggestion. You don't tell the administration shit. Let me just jimmy up one of the electrical plugs so this room can't be used. Then we'll move her. In the meantime, you get your ass moving to find her a new place. Me and the other nurses will ask around to the good homes and see if there's any availability. How about that?"

"Seems to me, there's a lot of smart in this room," Aliana said.

"Sure is, glad you recognize it," Shorinda grinned. "Now you work on your lying abilities. Tell me, is that your cop out there in the hall?"

"He's not my cop."

"So, he's up for grabs? Because that sure looks like something I wouldn't mind grabbing."

Aliana choked on a laugh. She was going to miss Shorinda when her mother moved to another nursing home. "Would you like me to introduce you?"

"Honey, I see the way he's looking over at this room. There isn't a chance in hell he's going to be interested in me. He only has eyes for you."

"He's just doing his job. And if he isn't, I'll get the message through to him."

Shorinda eyed her and then sighed. "Yes, I suppose you will."

* * *

"Officer Robinson, thank you for seeing me home." Aliana held out her hand.

"I told you my name is Ernie."

"Yes, well, let's just keep it formal, shall we?" Aliana waited for him to take her hand.

"You're stubborn."

"Yes," she agreed. He didn't know the half of it.

"The offer still stands for me to pick you up tomorrow. I told you it's my day off."

"That won't be necessary." Aliana searched him for any sign of irritation, but instead, he looked resigned. Good.

"I'm going to call you on Monday to see how you're doing."

"Officer, that really isn't necessary."

"Expect a call, Ms. Novak," he said with a smile. "Now I'm going to wait here until you lock your door."

Aliana went inside her townhome, shut the door, and immediately locked it.

"I'll call you on Monday," Ernie called from the other side of the door.

"Thank you for everything."

"Stay safe."

Aliana strode through the large living room straight back to her bedroom, turning on every light as she went. She stripped as soon as she got to the master bathroom, wanting to ignore the bathroom mirror as usual, but this time she couldn't. She needed to check to see that her chest and throat bandages were secure before she took a shower. She took in her appearance. Yep, it was the same—long, straw-colored hair that was better left pinned to the top of her head, blue eyes too big for her face, and skin which looked washed out.

Her gaze drifted lower to her right thigh. There they were. The scars. She looked up at the bandage on her chest and throat, now. she would have more to add to the collection.

She sighed, it really didn't matter how many scars she collected, it wasn't as if anybody who mattered would see them, she'd made sure of that. She traced one of the lines on her thighs. It reminded her of so many things, her emotions were so high tonight. Aliana snatched her hand away, trembling as she examined her bandages and determined they were fine for the shower.

She turned the shower on as hot as she could stand it. She needed to wipe away those moments of fear. She hated the feeling of desperation and swore she could actually smell the stench of despair.

She closed her eyes, letting the hot water pelt the top of her head, praying it would wash her clean, wash away the memories of schoolyard terror.

"You're stronger than this."

But she wasn't.

Images like the water washed over her.

* * *

"I didn't tell teacher."

"Lupita said you did."

Aliana didn't know what to do when he shoved her in the chest. She teetered on her toes, trying to keep from falling down.

Lupita and Heather giggled. "Push her down in the dirt, Jose," Lupita egged on her older brother.

"Push her. Push her. Push her." Heather's singsong voice grated on Aliana's ears.

"You snitched to the teacher." He punched her in her shoulder, and she crashed to the ground.

"Kick her. Kick her. Kick her." This time it was Lupita.

"Please, stop," Aliana said in Czech. So scared, she couldn't come up with the words in English.

"Listen to the dummy, she's talkin' foreign." Heather laughed.

Aliana started to cry. Why were they being mean to her? She didn't understand it. Heather was supposed to be her friend. They'd been friends since preschool. They went to church together.

"You snitched," Jose said again.

She didn't understand. She shook her head wildly. "I did no wrong."

Heather knelt down beside her and grabbed her hair. "You told the teacher that Lupita cheated off your paper. You're a snitch."

"I didn't tell teacher."

"Liar!" Lupita yelled.

"I—"

Lupita shoved a fistful of dirt into her open mouth, choking her. The little girl slammed her two little hands over Aliana's nose and mouth, smothering her. Aliana clawed at Lupita's fingers, her wrists, anything she could reach, but she couldn't stop her. She bucked and kicked her legs, but she couldn't get either Heather or Lupita to release her. She heard laughter.

Why was this happening? She hadn't told teacher that Lupita copied. She never told teacher anything. Tears mixed with the dirt. Now mud filled her mouth.

"Ooof."

Pain shot through her as Lupita's elbow struck her chin. Aliana was loose, she scrabbled away from her tormentor, spitting the dirt and mud out of her mouth. She couldn't get too far because Heather still had hold of her long hair.

"She's getting away," Heather cried.

Now Aliana could see more clearly, she saw a boy sitting astride Jose, hitting him. Lupita was trying to drag him off her brother. Aliana took the opportunity to grab her hair and yank it out of Heather's hands.

"Now I tell teacher," she threatened.

"Dirty foreigner, she won't believe you," Heather laughed.

Aliana was on all fours. She couldn't stop her tears. It was true. Her teacher hated the way she talked. She was constantly correcting her in front of the other children. She only liked the way she wrote on the paper.

"—ever hit her again, I will beat you bloody." *Aliana looked up to see who had said that. It was a boy she recognized from the hallways. She thought he might be in fourth grade. Jose was in fifth. The boy had an odd name. He was a Hunter like in Snow White. He turned to Aliana.* "Go tell the teacher."

Aliana shook her head. Heather was right, they wouldn't believe her. The boy got off Jose and stood up. He looked around at the other two girls.

"If you ever touch her again, you'll answer to me."

Lupita looked scared, Heather smirked. It made no sense to Aliana. None of the children's actions that day made any sense. Not her friend, Heather, not Lupita and Jose, not even her rescuer. She stood there trying to stop crying. When she got back to school, she ran to the bathroom and wiped her face. When teacher asked her what was wrong, she said she fell down. Even the teacher's lack of interest made no sense. Aliana vowed to never do anything to bring attention to herself again. Too bad her actions had nothing to do with being a target for bullies.

* * *

Aliana shut off the shower and stepped out. It had been a long time since she had thought about her school days. Her hands trembled as she pulled on her soft pajamas. She hated remembering how powerless she had been. The memory must have surfaced because of how Mateo had made her feel.

She considered again whether she was doing the right thing not to go to the police. To begin with she wanted to save Nicolas, but when they threatened her mother, all of her faith in authority left her. If Mateo had been able to knock out her security cameras and know exactly what room her mother was in? She shuddered at his power. No, she couldn't risk it.

She got into bed and shoved the pillows behind her back. She crossed her legs and put her hands on her knees. She breathed in and held her breath for a count of three, then carefully released it for a count of ten. She did that twenty times until she finally felt herself begin to calm. She could stop counting her breaths and just ease into a state of being.

When she opened her eyes, she wasn't surprised to find her face was tight from dried tears, but she felt more relaxed. Not good exactly, but more centered. In control, that was it, she felt more in control. She uncurled and pushed the pillows away and turned out the light. It was a mistake.

She got up and went over to the plug on the wall and switched on her sunflower nightlight. She went back to her bed and wrapped her down comforter around herself and burrowed in. She stared at her nightlight until she finally slept.

* * *

"What *really* happened to you?" Lottie hissed.

They were sitting in the back corner of the teacher's lounge eating lunch. Aliana was tired of all the attention she had garnered that morning.

"I was in a car accident."

"Your car was fine. I checked it out." Carlotta Rodriguez peeled off the film from her microwaved diet meal and grimaced.

"I was in a friend's car," Aliana whispered back.

"You don't have any other friends but me. You're anti-social, remember?"

It was true.

"A new neighbor moved in," Aliana told her. "We were going to lunch, and she wrecked the car."

"You're such a bad liar."

It was getting frustrating that everybody doubted her word these days. She needed to work on her ability to deceive.

"Oh, my God, you're trying to think of ways to become a better liar!" Lottie hissed again. "Stop it. I'll tell your grandmother on you. By the way, that would have been a much better lie. You should have said she'd been driving."

"I had her license revoked a couple of years ago, remember?" She'd felt terrible, because they ended up having to sell her grandfather's car as well, and that was what hurt her Babička the most.

Lottie grimaced. "I forgot sweetie." She put her hand on top of Aliana's. "I remember how tough that was for you. But she had a good run, she's damn near eighty. Now tell me what really happened."

"I can't."

Aliana watched as Lottie morphed from her friend into the skilled school counselor who nurtured almost two thousand teenagers. Not only was Carlotta Rodriguez a counselor, she was a psychiatric social worker who provided both counseling and mental health services to the students at Bertrum High School. Since they were in the middle of Eastmont, which was rife with gangs, many of the students had families and friends who had been victims, or the students themselves had been victims of violence. When Carlotta had transferred to the school three years ago, she'd been a godsend. Except for those times when she decided to put Aliana under her psychiatric microscope. Aliana preferred it when they remained in the best friend category.

"We're going out to dinner," Lottie proclaimed.

"I have work to do."

"I'm sick of dieting." She held up a piece of something that resembled beef on her fork and waved it in front of Aliana's nose. "You know you've been telling me I need to kick this diet to the curb. Now's your chance to help me splurge," Lottie wheedled. Damn, the woman knew how to push her buttons. "You need to eat more too. You keep saying you want to put on some weight."

"Quit using your voodoo tactics on me."

"Comes with being my friend. I'm good for you." Lottie paused and gave her a kind smile. "Come on, you know I've never delved too deep."

That was true.

"Fine, we'll go to dinner," Aliana relented.

"Great."

"Now, I need to get back to my office."

"You didn't eat anything," Lottie protested.

"Please, don't nag. I would have, but…" she touched her throat. "It hurts to swallow."

"What did the doctor say about that?" Aliana looked down at her barely touched yogurt. "Dammit. You didn't discuss this with them, did you?"

Two of the teachers looked curiously at them as they left the room.

"Would you keep your voice down?" Aliana requested.

"No, I won't. You either go to the nurse's office, or we go to urgent care after school today. Those are your choices."

She didn't like either one of them. She glared at her friend. They were no longer best friends. Maybe they weren't even going to be friends anymore. She didn't need friends, did she?

"Stop having conversations in your head," Lottie sighed with exasperation. "Just give in."

"I wasn't—"

Lottie raised her eyebrow, and Aliana laughed.

She felt her purse vibrate. It must important, nobody called her during school hours unless it was an emergency. She pulled her phone out of her purse. It was an unknown number. She answered.

"Aliana?"

"This is Aliana Novak. May I help you?"

"This is Ernie Robinson. I was calling to find out how you're doing."

"I'm." Aliana swallowed to clear her throat, and it went down the wrong way, and she started coughing. She couldn't believe he was calling her, and she couldn't seem to stop coughing. Lottie was looking at her with concern.

"Aliana? What's going on? Are you alright? Do you need to go back to the hospital?" Ernie asked.

"No," she gasped out. This was ridiculous. "I'm fine," she wheezed, then coughed again.

"Aliana, you don't sound fine." He was speaking loudly enough to be heard over her coughing, Lottie heard him.

"Give me the phone." She held out her hand. Aliana jerked it away from her friend. The last thing she needed was these two talking.

"Who's that?" Ernie asked. "Let me talk to her," he demanded.

"I heard that," Lottie reached over the table, somehow managing not to plant her right breast into the blackberry yogurt while still grabbing the phone out of her hand.

"How did you do that?" Aliana gasped.

"Who is this?" Lottie asked.

"I'm Ernie Robison. I'm with the L.A.P.D.," Aliana heard him say.

"How do you do? I'm Aliana's best friend. She didn't tell me you would be calling," Lottie said sweetly. Aliana got up from the chair and went over to the vending machine, coughing the entire way. Her water bottle was empty. She had no choice but to get something to drink to stop this sudden fit. She felt all eyes in the lounge on her, the last thing she wanted.

Scratch that. Her eyes narrowed as she saw Lottie all comfortable with her phone. *Sakra*, that was the last thing she needed. She pinched the bridge of her nose as she sat back down.

"No, Ernie, she's not all right. We're going to the urgent care right after school. I'm worried about her trachea or her larynx."

There was a pause. Then there it was. She hit him with it. Ernie would be shutting down.

"I'm a psychiatrist. I went to medical school." The conversation would be over with.

Lottie listened, then burst out laughing. "Yep, that's me, right down to a tee. If they say her throat is just swollen and nothing is really damaged, do you want to join us for some wedding soup and enchiladas? Girlfriend and I need to eat."

Again, there was a pause.

"Great. I'll call you." Lottie handed back her phone. "Is he as hot as he sounds?"

"Huh?"

"Ernie? He sounds dreamy."

"Dreamy? Did you just say dreamy? You've been spending too much time with the students." Aliana closed the lid on her yogurt, gathered up her banana and threw them into her paper sack.

"I'll be in your office at three-thirty. I'll make an appointment for you at four."

"That's too early. I have work to do." Lottie followed her to the trash can and out the door.

"Don't make me talk to Roger. He'll back me up."

She would too, Lottie would definitely go to the principal.

"Fine," Aliana sighed. "I'll go to urgent care. I'll give you a call when I get home and tell you how it went."

Lottie smiled and shook her head. Aliana knew that gesture. She wasn't getting out of having a shadow at her appointment.

"I'll see you at three-thirty."

* * *

Not again. This was the third time she'd been called to the music room, and she was sick of it. This was Breanne Clarke's first year on the job, and she was going through a trial by fire. She was a gifted music teacher, but unfortunately, there were three senior boys in the class who were taking it for easy credit to graduate. They were unmanageable, and Ms. Clark didn't have the slightest clue how to discipline them. Today had to take the cake.

Aliana wrenched open one of the double doors, and it swung open and slammed. Holy hell, it had a broken hinge. Well, fine, she figured it didn't hurt her reputation to make an entrance as all eyes were riveted to her, including the three senior boys.

"You three. Here. Now." She pointed at Lucky, Carlos, and David and pointed to the floor in front of her.

"Who?" Lucky asked.

"You make me repeat myself, this will escalate from suspension to expulsion."

David, who was the weak link, stood up and gave a pleading look to his compatriots. Carlos stood up. Lucky put his feet up on the back seat of the girl in front of him. She shoved them off. "Fucker," Aliana heard her mumble.

"She's bluffing," Lucky said to his friends. "Sit your asses down."

"Lucky, congratulations. You've hit the suspension trifecta. This time I'll call your dad over at the plant."

He sat up in his chair. "You can't suspend me. You haven't heard my side."

"I can. I am. You're out. David and Carlos quit dragging your feet."

She watched as they double-timed it down the stairs to stand in front of her. "Tell me what happened."

Carlos got a sly look on his face and looked up at a stunned Lucky. "It was his idea," he said, pointing to his friend.

"Isn't that convenient," Aliana drawled. "Tell me the truth." She used her voice like a whip. "Who put the animal excrement in the tubas?"

"What?" David said.

There was murmured laughter in the music room. Breanne turned red.

"Yeah, I don't understand?" Carlos said innocently.

"Feces?" Breanne said helpfully.

"Breanne, they understand the word. They're the ones who filled the tubas full of dogshit. Now they will clean them out, then pay for a professional cleaning, and David and Carlos will be suspended for three days. Meanwhile, Mr. Unlucky will be suspended for a week, and kicked out of your class permanently with a failing grade."

"You can't do that. I need this grade, otherwise, I have to go to summer school," Lucky whined.

"Should have done what I asked you to, now shouldn't you? Lucky, do you want to try for expulsion, or are you going to kindly join your friends down here with me, and we all take a nice walk to my office?"

She watched as the student got up and walked toward her. He looked like he had been poked with a cattle prod.

Good, her job was done.

* * *

So bright and shiny, how could he be related to Mateo? Nicolas Garcia stood in front of her, excitedly waving his essay in front of her.

"Ms. Dunbar submitted it to the Library of Congress six months ago for their literacy contest! It's a finalist," he cried. There were tears in his eyes. Nicolas was big at fifteen, already bigger than his brother and a lot smarter. Why couldn't Mateo leave him alone? She hated that Nicolas' brother was so intent on dragging him into *Los Demonios*. She hated that name. She hated their logo, even more, the picture of the demon was so evil looking, it made her shiver every time she saw it, not that she would ever admit it.

"Nicolas, that is excellent."

"I think you had something to do with it," he said astutely.

"The selection was made on merit," she assured him.

"I mean the contest. They didn't do that last year. It was your idea to have them submit our papers, wasn't it?"

Yep, smart. His smile faded.

"What happened to you, Ms. Novak? Why are you wearing a bandage?"

She looked him straight in the eye, and said, "I was in a small car wreck this weekend."

He looked at her for three heartbeats, then asked, "Are you going to be okay?"

"Of course, it was a minor accident. The doctor said I was fine."

His brown eyes darkened. "The school can't afford to have something happen to you, you need to take care of yourself."

"We were talking about you," she smiled. "Tell me more about your paper."

"It was on George Orwell. I had to write him a letter and tell him how his book, Animal Farm, impacted me."

Aliana had already read his paper, Glenda had shown it to her before submitting it.

He paused, clearly uncomfortable. He looked behind him, making sure no one was outside her door who could overhear him.

"Do you want to shut the door?"

He stood up straight. "No," he said, all bravado.

"So, tell me about your paper. I'm excited to hear about," her emphasis *hear*. She was dying to hear his take on why he had written it.

He leaned in. "Animal Farm talks about how fear is used to make people conform. It's kind of what *Los Demonios* does. There are a lot of the same dynamics. You know?"

Boy, did she know. She nodded her head.

"You have to shake off the shackles. I want to be like Snowball."

"What do you mean? You want to be like the pig who started the revolution on the farm?"

"Exactly. A lot of the kids who join the gang do it because they want to be part of something, they do it for a sense of brotherhood. They don't realize just how evil it is before it's too late. That's exactly like what happens in the book." She knew she had never been this zealous about anything, not even her poetry or music.

She took out voice Number Thirteen, the Kind, Firm and Fair voice. "Nicolas, you can't start a revolution. Your only task is to be a kid, do well in school, and get the hell out of the gang. Got it?"

"Snowball was scared too, but he had to do it, Ms. Novak. You do the right thing all the time. Everybody heard what you did in the music room. You were righteous. I'm doing the same thing. With some help."

"Nicolas, what you're suggesting is too dangerous."

"Don't worry," he gave her a pitying look, "I was born into it Ms. Novak."

"But you're not part of it."

"Of course, I am. My family is. It's all around me. I'm one of them."

"What do you mean your family? I thought it was just your brother?"

"Never mind. I just try to keep my head down. I hope you're right, and I get to leave and go to college."

If it took her dying breath, he'd get out of here, she swore to herself.

"With your abilities, of course, you will, Nicolas."

"Do you think this contest will help?"

"It helped me. Did I tell you I went to school in Boyle Heights?"

"No way!" he exclaimed. "I thought you were all that. You were one of us? A homegirl?"

"Not exactly a homegirl," she smiled. "I talked with an accent, was overweight, and dressed funny, I hardly fit in."

"You sure came a long way," he said with admiration.

"Thank you."

"Was it tough for you?" he asked. Smart and perceptive.

"It wasn't easy."

"I'm sorry."

"It was a long time ago. Still—" She waved her hand. "We're talking about you. I just wanted you to know there is a way out. I won a national contest in poetry. People noticed me, and I got a scholarship. It's possible, Nicolas. Never give up on your dreams. Okay?"

He raked his fingers through his black hair. She had a flashback to another boy who used to do the exact same thing. She slammed that door shut. Then he flashed a grin, and the door flew open and pain made her bleed. Nicolas even had dimples.

"I won't. I'll never give up on my dreams."

"Promise?"

"I promise. But Ms. Novak, there are some others who are worthy of dreams too. I have to do my best to save them."

"No," she said vehemently. "Nicolas, it's too dangerous."

"I can't live with myself if I don't try. Don't worry about me, I know what I'm doing. Remember this has been my life forever." He looked down at his paper, and his grin exploded. "Thanks again."

"Thanks for what?" Lottie asked.

Nicolas started and spun around. He relaxed when he saw the school counselor. "Oh, hi Dr. Rodriguez."

"Hi, Nicolas. Are you staying out of trouble," she asked, her eyes sparkling.

"Are you kidding? I wouldn't dare piss off Ms. Novak."

"That sounds about right. How's Darla?"

It was as if all the air got sucked out of the room. Aliana shot her friend a dark look. Lottie ignored her.

"She's doing okay," he mumbled.

"She should stop by my office. I miss our talks."

"She doesn't go here anymore," he said, surprised.

"Doesn't matter. My door is open to former students. She's special."

He considered her words. "I'll tell her. Look, I've got to go." He brushed past her on the way out of the office.

"Dammit Lottie, why did you do that?" Aliana demanded.

"I know Nicolas is one of your pets, well Darla is just as important," Lottie said fiercely.

Aliana disagreed. The girl had attempted to stab a freshman a year and a half ago and ended up in juvenile detention for eight months. She'd been out for the last six months and was now pregnant. The girl had been a bully the first day she stepped foot in Bertrum High, and she consistently escalated. Aliana had been a hairsbreadth from expelling her before the attempted stabbing had taken place.

Her fault. Totally her fault Kevin had almost been stabbed. If she'd just gotten Darla out of the school sooner.

"I know that look. Stop it. You followed the process. Neither of us knew she was that desperate."

"She wasn't desperate. Quit saying that. She's vicious."

"You just can't see past her actions to what motivates her. A lot of pain and abuse made her that way."

"Nicolas and she grew up in the same house. They couldn't be any more different. How do you explain that?" Aliana scoffed.

Lottie shook her head. "When it comes to some students, there's no reasoning with you. It's what keeps you from making the leap from great to exceptional."

Aliana sighed. "Did you come here for a reason?"

"It's time to leave. You have an appointment, remember?"

Aliana glanced up at the clock on the wall. Where had the day gone?

"At least I know talking isn't hurting you anymore."

"Arguing with you always comes easy."

"We don't argue. We debate. Get your stuff. The sooner we get a diagnosis, the closer I am to meeting Cop-o-licious."

"Seriously? You can't be serious. You're a grown woman, right?"

"Sex on a stick?" Lottie asked innocently as they walked out of her office.

"Keep your voice down."

"He has a great ass, doesn't he?"

God, she was going to need a fireman to put out the flames on her face. Lottie was outrageous, and it continued all the way out into the teacher's parking lot.

"Are you telling me you didn't pick up on one physical attribute on our erstwhile knight in shining in armor?"

"See, that's the problem. There is no such thing."

"Sure there is. You're one. I've watched you be a savior to hundreds of kids. Why wouldn't there be someone who is a white knight for you?" Lottie asked.

Aliana turned to look at her friend. "It's a fairy tale."

"No, I'm serious. I've met some really good men in my life. My husband was one of those men before the wreck that killed him."

"I wish I could have met him," Aliana said not for the first time.

"I wish you could have too. But that was another time, another place." Lottie shook off her sadness and smiled. "Who knows, cop-o-licious might be another one of the good ones."

Aliana rolled her eyes, then hit her key fob to unlock her car. "I'll meet you at the doctor's office."

"Well, don't be late."

"You do realize you're a nag, don't you?"

"Honey, you might not believe in a knight in shining armor, so instead you have a fairy godmother watching over you. That'd be me."

Aliana wasn't sure she even believed in that.

* * *

That evening when she went to bed, she saw her nightlight still on and smiled sadly. She'd had a knight once. He'd given her a sunflower and a saint necklace to watch over her, to keep her from being lonely. She remembered that day like it was yesterday. It was the day before Hunter Diaz was going to leave forever.

"I'm not going to leave you forever. I'll write you letters. I'll visit."

Aliana picked at her ankle-length cotton skirt. The one that had gotten so much negative attention that day at school. They were in the backyard of her grandparent's house, sitting on the old swing set her grandfather had put up for her before he'd died.

Hunter didn't say anything. She looked up, he was staring at her intently.

She hugged her stomach, she knew it pooched out.

"Don't do that," he said angrily.

She hunched over further, looking down at the grass.

"Alia, I think you're perfect the way you are. You never have to hide from me. You have to know that."

He'd said that a lot over the years. He always tried to make her feel better, especially when she would show him the pictures somebody drew of her. She hadn't shown him anything or told him stuff since he found her under the bleachers.

"You know I have to go? Don't you?"

She nodded her head, her hair heavy in a bun. She wore it that way so nobody could pull it. Her parents wouldn't allow her to cut it. Some of it got loose, and Hunter brushed it back behind her ear. Her head jerked up to look at him.

"You have the prettiest hair."

"I do?" she asked, her Czech accent thick.

"Yes," he smiled. Hunter's smile made her think of one of her favorite songs because it made her heart happy. He didn't do it often, but when he did, it showed the creases in his cheeks. He would hate it if she called them dimples.

"You and Mamie are the only reasons for me to stay, but I have to leave, you understand that, don't you?"

She shook her head, but saw his dismay, so she quickly nodded.

It hurt, but she gave her best smile possible.

"It's okay Hunter, I'll be fine," she lied.

He sighed. "I have something for you."

She frowned. He pulled out a small box from his beat-up backpack and handed it to her. Her hands trembled. Hunter was giving her a gift. She was excited but scared. She hadn't thought to give him anything.

"I don't have—"

He laughed. "Chaquita, just open it."

It wasn't wrapped, just a brown box. Inside was a sunflower. She picked it up with reverent fingers.

"You remind me of sunflowers. They grow through the pavement and are strong and pretty, like you."

She huffed out a breath. "I'm not strong. I'm weak. That's why you have to take care of me."

"I hear things. There's a lot you don't tell me. You live with a lot of abuse. Yet you still manage to come to school every day no

matter what those bitches do. I admire you more than anyone else I know."

She didn't understand him. He was the brave one. He was the one who was going to be a soldier, and he thought she was strong? He was crazy.

"No," she said in Czech, then realized her mistake. "You're wrong, Hunter." She hated it when she sounded foreign. When she said as much, he smiled.

"I like how you talk. It's different. It's cute."

"You're acting odd," she accused.

"It's because I won't see you for a long time. I needed you to know I'm going to miss you. Look at what else is in the box. I looked it up in one of Mamie's books and went to a special store to buy it for you."

She pulled a delicate gold chain with a gold medallion out of the box. It had a woman who looked like the Virgin Mary on it. "Is it the Blessed Mother?" she asked.

"You're so Catholic," he teased.

"So are you," she shot back.

"I just go to mass," he laughed. "That's Saint Rita, she takes away loneliness and protects women from abuse."

Aliana's eyes widened. She'd never heard of her. "Really?"

"Honest. Let me put it on you." He stood up from his seat and walked behind her. She watched in fascination as the medal dropped down in front of her, feeling it as he fastened the clasp at the back of her neck.

"There."

She lifted and turned it so she could look at it. She jumped up from her swing, dropping the box on the ground, but still gripping her flower firmly in her hand, then flung her arms around Hunter.

"This is the best present I ever got. Thank you. Thank you."

He laughed. "You're welcome."

At the sound of his laughter, Aliana realized what she had done, and released him, stumbling backward. He caught her before she fell.

"Hey, what's going on?"

"I shouldn't have hugged you."

"Sure you should have, how else would I have known you liked the present?"

He totally confused her.

"Sit back down. I have one more thing for you."

She sat back down on the swing, and he crouched down in front of her and pulled an envelope out of his pocket. "Can you promise me, not to read this until after I leave?"

"I don't understand. Why?"

"Just promise, okay." He took her hand and wrapped it around the envelope. "Swear."

She looked into his intent brown eyes, "I swear to God, Hunter."

"Thank you."

Aliana pulled the long chain from around her neck and pulled up the St. Rita medal, staring at it for long minutes. She had bought the chain after she'd been teased about the medallion. Now, she was glad because it rested against her heart. Aliana went to her dresser and took her Bible out of her drawer, opening it to the page where her sunflower was pressed. She stroked it with her finger before putting it back. She opened up her purse and pulled out a lined paper out of her wallet, Hunter's letter. His bold printing was faded from all the times she had touched the words. She read it once again, then again, and put it back, too. Her ritual complete, she got back under the covers.

"It's a dream. A dream," she said in Czech. "There are no knights for you. You are nothing but a responsibility that kills men's dreams."

CHAPTER THREE

Two days later, she was still thinking about knights and fairies. It seemed they attracted one another, and it was a bright spot in her day to think about it. Aliana had gone and visited her mother. Today had been a red-letter day. Her mother had recognized her when she was brushing her hair.

"Love," she said in Czech. "You should wear your hair down, it's so pretty."

Aliana had to fight back tears. She'd never told her mother why she'd started wearing her hair up. Now, it was habit. Her mother had hated it up. She loved Aliana's hair, called it her crowning glory.

"I know it's pretty, it's because it's like yours, Mama."

"Take it down," she asked. "I want to see it."

"Sure." If doing that little thing would bring a smile to Danica Novak's face, she would do it. Hell, she'd do cartwheels if her mother asked. She pulled out the bobby pins holding it up, then bent at the waist and ran her fingers through it before swinging her head backward. She had to admit, she always felt better when the weight of her hair wasn't on her head. It felt good loose.

"You're beautiful."

"Thank you, Mama, but you're biased." She picked up the brush again and started to softly brush her mother's fine white hair.

"Can you put lotion on?"

"Sure can."

She opened up the drawer beside the bed. "What kind, Mama?"

"Rose."

She took out the rose lotion and was assaulted by the smell. Images flashed in front of her face. So much blood. She shoved it down. Down. She was here with her mother, she needed to concentrate on the here and now.

"That feels so good," her mother said when she rubbed the moisturizer into her palms and fingers. "I'm tired now, Baby."

"I love you, Mama."

"You're my beautiful girl. Always remember, Love. You're beautiful."

Damn, she was going to lose it. Her mother was so kind and good. She didn't deserve this life.

"Why are you crying, Aliana? Where's your father? Tell him to come here."

These were the worst moments when her mother asked for her dead husband. "You rest, Mama, I'll go get him. Okay?"

Experience told her that these moments of lucidity wouldn't last long, and when she woke up, she wouldn't remember their conversation. It was best just to pacify her. It was good that her mom remembered the Lazlo Novak from their younger years together, and not like he was when Aliana was a teenager. Back then he hadn't been exactly happy, but he'd had dreams. He had his poetry. He hadn't crashed over the cliff into true bitterness yet.

"Thank you, Baby. I don't like sleeping alone."

Aliana choked back a sob, for her mother and herself. She hated thinking of the way her father had left them. She hated the confusion and the pain he caused with his suicide. Mostly, she was dead tired from the sorrow his last words had brought to her life.

"He's coming," she lied to her mother. "Can I sing to you until he arrives?"

"That would be wonderful. Get the guitar."

Aliana knew that when the dark mire of ugly memories poured over her, music was a savior for her. Music had always been important in their house growing up, so there were many lullabies for her to choose from. Her mother had often played her guitar while either she or her grandmother had sung to her. She pulled the guitar out of the cupboard. She had bought it for times just like these. She knew it was in tune because she had played last week.

"What song would you like, Mama?"

"One of yours."

It took Aliana a moment to think of one she felt like singing. She had to settle her mind. Finally, she thought of the perfect one, something to celebrate life. She had written it six years ago when her mother had first moved in with her. She knew her mother's mind was starting to go, so she wanted to honor her and the caring woman she had been while raising Aliana. She called it simply, *Danica*.

My Mother raised me up
Shouldering my burdens
Wiping My Tears
My Mother Loved Me
So, I Stand Strong Today

Danica's Love Blessed Me
She Raised Me Up High
Danica's Love Is Clear to See
It Lifts Up To the Sky

Her Arms Gave Comfort
Into them, I ran
Always she provided solace
My Mother Loved Me
So, I Stand Strong Today

Danica's Love Blessed Me
She Raised Me Up High
Danica's Love Is Clear to See
It Lifts Up To the Sky

She sang another couple of Czech lullabies and her mother fell asleep.

Shorinda wasn't working that night, so she said goodnight to the night nurse on duty. She stopped by Trader Joe's on the way home. It was the first time she'd gotten groceries since she'd been attacked. She waited to get out of her car until one of her neighbors, Lester Nuñez, pulled into the parking lot and gave a sigh of relief. Okay, now she could go to her house.

Instead of focusing on the fact that she'd waited in her car for eighteen minutes for someone to show up, she decided to focus on the good. She'd gotten to talk to her mom. She swung her Trader Joe's shopping bags out of the trunk and thought about Ernie and Lottie. They were quite the pair. Sparks had flown from the second they had sat across from one another at the restaurant.

Fumbling with her lock, she dropped one of her grocery bags. The tomatoes rolled out and she dumped the other bag and started after her fruit when she was catapulted into the air. A dragon roared fire over her head and then something hit her back. Fire. What? Black.

"Can you hear me?"

Leave me alone. Why wouldn't he leave her alone? She tried to slap his hands away.

Oww. Don't pull on my eyelids. Hurts. Light hurts.

"Stop that." Where was her crisp vice principal voice?

"She's conscious."

"Course am," she slurred.

"Pupils look good."

"That door saved her."

Tired. "Sleep now," she said.

Everything went black again.

* * *

Aliana woke up to the sound of a different Czech lullaby. She couldn't stop the tears. She was in pain and remembered enough of the conversations around her last night to know her townhome had blown up.

"Mama?" she asked in Czech.

"It's me, your grandmother, Love," Her grandmother answered in the same language.

Aliana recognized her voice. She should have from the song.

"Aliana, my darling girl. How are you feeling?" Aliana opened her eyes and saw her grandmother. She looked like a dowager queen in her long black dress, white lace collar, and perfect posture.

She looked around and realized she was in a private hospital room. *Sakra*. Okay, this deserved worse. Fuck. She ground her teeth and felt pain, a lot, and moaned.

Her grandmother rose from her chair, bent over the bed, and cupped her cheek. "What can I do to make this better for you?"

Aliana placed her hand over her grandmother's fragile hand. "Just having you here helps."

"If that is true, why am I not your emergency contact?" Her grandmother arched an eyebrow.

Fuck. *Sakra*. She was so busted.

"How did you find out I was here?" Lottie had so lost her best friend status.

"Your home blew up. Don't you think I would have heard about it?" came the spry reply.

"But from who?" Aliana persisted.

"Ultimately, it was Mrs. Lasson who told me, but that was three hours after it happened. Why didn't the police inform me immediately? Tell me why I'm not your emergency contact. You're mine."

"Ah, grandmother, I just never want to worry you," she said softly. She hated thinking of her wonderful grandmother getting a call in the middle of the night if something happened to her. Better if Lottie contacted her.

"I don't want to find out you were in the hospital three days after you're out. Or, God forbid, the day of your funeral." Her voice sounded like it had been grated through a shredder.

She pressed her grandmother's warm hand closer to her cheek. "I'm so sorry," her voice trembled. "Please, forgive me."

"I'll only let this slide because you're hurting, but as soon as you're on your feet, you have to put me in your phone. In the meantime, tell me what's going on. Why does somebody want you dead?"

"What are you talking about? It must have been a gas leak."

"I've talked to the detectives in charge of the investigation and Officer Robinson. They say a bomb was planted in your apartment."

All the blood left her body. How could she be alive if her blood was gone?

"Aliana, what's wrong? Nurse! Come immediately," her grandmother cried, switching to English.

A nurse followed by Lottie and Ernie came into the room. The nurse immediately looked up at the monitors. "Your blood pressure has gone up significantly. Can you calm down?"

"Ernie, was my townhome bombed?"

"Yeah, Honey, it was. Do you have any idea who might have wanted to do such a thing?"

She looked down at the blanket and shook her head.

"She's lying." Lottie and her grandmother said at the same time.

"Yeah, I got that," Ernie said wryly. "She does that a lot."

"No, she doesn't. My Aliana is a good girl." Her grandmother slapped Ernie on his arm.

"Tell your good girl to tell the truth then. We need to capture the men who want her dead."

Breathe and keep calm. Aliana watched dispassionately as the nurse studied her blood pressure. "It's better." The nurse proclaimed. "How are you feeling?"

"Do I need to be here?"

"The doctor wants you in here overnight for observation. You have a bad concussion. As long as you have someone that can stay with you, you can probably go home tomorrow."

"She can stay with me." Again, Lottie and her grandmother almost spoke in one voice.

"I don't need to stay with anyone."

"Really, where do you plan to live?" Ernie asked.

Aliana's shoulders drooped.

"Look on the bright side Chica, you never got that cat I kept telling you to adopt."

Aliana swallowed back bile, thinking about the cat she had stroked at the animal shelter. She had never told Lottie, but she had considered getting the beautiful Siamese, but something had held her back. It had seemed like too much of a commitment.

"We just need someone to watch over her for a couple of days. They should stay with her the entire time," a new voice said.

Aliana looked up to see a man who she assumed was a doctor, walk into her crowded room.

"That would be me," her grandmother said. "Carlotta has to go to work."

"I can take time off," Lottie protested.

"How soon before I can go back to work?" Aliana asked the doctor.

"You should be fine by next week, barring any complications," he answered.

"What should I be on the lookout for?" her grandmother asked.

"I'll give you a printout."

He came over and listened to Aliana's heart, then looked at her pupils. "You were very lucky you landed in the grass and the door wasn't the best quality. I would say God was looking over you."

"Except for the part that someone put a bomb in her house," Lottie said angrily.

"Aliana, there are two detectives who are going to want to talk to you tomorrow," Ernie said. "You need to be straight with them."

She looked at her grandmother, who looked so much like her mother. She couldn't. She just couldn't put her mother at risk. It was a miracle Mateo hadn't targeted her treasured *Babička*. But she didn't know what she was going to do. Was she going to have to give up on Nicolas in order to keep her mother safe? God, please help her find an answer she prayed.

"What are you thinking?" Lottie asked.

"What?"

"I don't like that expression on your face," her friend said.

"I think it's time for my patient to get some rest." The doctor started to usher everyone out.

"What time will she be discharged?" Ernie asked.

"About one o'clock."

"The detectives will be here about noon."

"I'll be here at eleven with some clothes and your grandmother."

"*Babička*, how did you get here?" Aliana asked her grandmother.

"I took a cab." God save her from stubborn women.

"Don't do that again. Call someone," Aliana said fiercely. Damn, now her throat and her head hurt.

"Oh, I'll call someone," her grandmother assured her. It sounded like a threat.

"Out," the doctor commanded.

She watched as everyone paraded out of her room. *Sakra*, she needed a plan and fast.

* * *

Hunter Diaz was dismantling his rifle when his lieutenant walked over to him.

"That was damn fine shooting. You've been getting in extra practice."

"Maybe."

"You've been pretty quiet since the mission in Cameroon. Is there anything you want to talk about?" Gray asked quietly.

Hunter shook his head, focusing on packing away his equipment.

"Let me phrase this another way. I think you and I should grab a beer."

Shit. As much as he respected Grayson Tyler, the last thing he needed was for the man to be poking around in his head.

"Gray, I really appreciate the thought, but I've dealt with it. Griff and I have talked. I think it hit him harder since he has a baby girl and all."

"That's what I would have thought, too. But he's not the one who's shut down, you are. It's either a beer or the shrink. Your choice."

Fuck.

"A beer sounds great."

Gray grinned and Hunter grimaced. His phone rang. He pulled it out of his duffel and blanched. He'd missed four calls from his grandmother.

"Grandmother?" he said in Spanish.

"Come home," his adopted grandmother said without preamble.

"What's wrong?" he clipped out his question, his gut in knots.

"I need you home now."

"Answer my question." He ignored Gray's intense regard.

"Have some respect, and just do what I say."

"*Mamie*," he growled.

"Fine. It's Aliana. She's in big trouble. Someone blew up her home last night. She almost died. The police aren't helping. But if you don't care. Don't come home." She hung up.

He looked down at his phone.

"Motherfucker!"

"That's a lot of anger for a man who just got done talking to his grandmother," Gray mused.

"Yeah, well, most men don't have Rosa Diaz as a grandmother." He stopped folding and started shoving shit into his duffel. Fuck it all.

"Why d'you call her *Mamie*? Why not *Abuelita*?"

"She's only half Mexican. Her mother's family is Haitian. *Mamie* is French for grandmother." He zipped up his bag, slung it over his shoulder, then stared at Gray.

"Well, that explains why you speak French so well," Gray murmured to himself. He watched Hunter zip up his duffel. "Going somewhere?" Gray asked blandly.

"I'm officially requesting leave."

"How long?"

"Fuck if I know."

Gray put his hand on Hunter's shoulder. "Can you listen to me a moment? Really listen?"

Hunter looked at his lieutenant. In the six years he'd been under the man's command, he'd only been this somber outside of a mission four times.

"Yes," Hunter said solemnly.

"I can tell something serious is going on up in L.A., but I think your response might be a little over the top."

"You don't understand."

"I know I don't, but hear me out."

Hunter nodded.

"You were just talking to the woman who you consider your grandmother, then said 'fuck' three times. That's not you. I think this shit with the kidnapped and raped girls in Africa got deep inside your heart, mind, and soul and you haven't dealt. If you don't, whatever is going on in L.A. is going to blow up in your face."

"With all due respect, Gray, you don't know fuck all what triggered me. And maybe, just maybe, going to L.A. will be just the thing to finally put this to rest."

Gray stared into his eyes. He must have seen something that reassured him. "Take your time then."

* * *

A week at most. *Mamie* had a washing machine he could use. Hell, at this rate, he'd have space left over in his saddlebags. Too bad his rifle wouldn't fit, But he had packed plenty of extras. Never hurt to be armed when going into enemy territory, and this was enemy fucking territory with a capital 'F'.

Hating the idea of any extra space, he packed his body armor. Being a SEAL meant you were a boy scout on steroids. Satisfied, he headed toward the door. He took one last look at his plants. Plants. Who would have guessed it? Thank God for Dex's cousin, she kept them alive. Of course, the little brat was the reason he had all of them, too. He locked up his apartment and went to his detached garage where his baby was, an Indian Springfield motorcycle, all black and chrome. She'd been needing a long drive. Hell, so had he.

He'd drive Pacific Coast Highway, wherever he could, on his way up to East L.A. It would help put his head on straight. He should have done this three months ago when he'd gotten back from the mission in Africa.

Elise. Her pretty voice, whispering horrific things to him in French, telling him what those fuckers had been doing to her and the other orphan girls. It still pissed him off he hadn't killed more of the Boko Haram fucks. Hunter took some deep breaths of the fresh ocean air as he pulled out onto PCH. Bike was running so smooth, she purred. It was almost worth a smile. Almost.

Pictures fluttered through his mind. Black girls, abused by adult men, white girls abused by playground bullies, then by teenage bitches—no matter what, they were all hurting. All victims. Each girl evoked the same emotions in him. The need to protect. The need was ingrained at the cellular level, especially when it came to females.

Gray had been right, the mission had chewed him up, but not for the reason he thought. It had stirred long-buried memories. A time when he thought he'd been doing something worthwhile. Hell, his Alia had made him feel like a nine-foot-tall hero instead of a nine-year-old nothing. Then it had all gone wrong. He still didn't know how it could have changed. She had meant everything to him. She had been the best thing in his life outside of *Mamie* since the third grade, then it just ended.

A little past Laguna Beach, he waved back to the three kids in the back of the SUV who were impressed by a guy on a bike. *Concentrate on the road.* But that was the problem, he'd always been able to concentrate on six things at once. It's why he'd excelled during his time in the *Las Nuevas Espadas* gang and still managed to graduate school with a high enough grade point to be considered for the SEAL teams when he joined the Navy. Hell, the hardest thing had been making time to go to the community pool at the rec center. Why the hell did one of the toughest of the tough all of a sudden need to learn how to swim?

Hunter grinned. The look on Red Blade's face when he said he was planning on surfing to impress the ladies had been a sight to behold. The gang leader and his lieutenants thought he was so funny, they just let it pass that he was going to the pool three days a week. Nobody, not *Mamie*, nobody in the gang, none of the teachers at school, not even his Alia had an inkling of his plan. Nobody except the man who had guided him toward it.

When he had to get on the Ten freeway to head toward downtown. Hunter decided to reward himself with a double-double burger and fries from In-and-Out Burger. The place he stopped wasn't a bad neighborhood, but he still gave everyone a stare as he got off his bike to go in to place his order. His bike was in the same pristine shape he'd left it. He sat down at a cement table under a red and white umbrella and chewed his food. He still wasn't in the right head space to face home. Hell, would he ever be?

He thought about how he last saw Aliana. It was three days after her father had committed suicide. She had been so distant, and all he wanted to do was wrap his arms around her and tell her everything would be okay.

He'd stayed at *Mamie*'s for three days and only had a chance to see her twice. The first time had been at her grandmother's house after the service at the cemetery. Mamie was with him. Both of them went and paid their respects to Mrs. Novak and Mrs. Jancovik, and standing between them was Aliana. She wouldn't look at him. Eventually, he found her in the backyard alone on the swing.

He touched her hand, and she jerked it away. She stumbled out of the swing as she stood up to stand over him. She told him to go away. She didn't want to see him anymore. She said that she was relieving him of all responsibility. She was never going to be a burden to him again. It had made no fucking sense. Before he could even figure out how to respond, her grandmother rushed out, put her arm around Aliana, and told him to leave.

He hadn't left it at that, he had snuck into her bedroom the following night. She was sitting up in bed with her Bible when he climbed through her unlocked window. She watched him do it without saying a word.

"Talk to me Alia, you have to talk to me. We've been writing letters for a year. I've told you things I've never told another living soul. How can you just tell me to go away?"

She stared through him.

She was wearing a pink flannel nightgown with lace at the throat. Her hair was down like it used to be in grade school, flowing around her face. Her skin was like porcelain. She looked at him with sky blue eyes, devoid of emotion.

"You should leave."

"What is that shit about 'relieving me of responsibility?' You weren't making any kind of sense yesterday, Chaquita."

"Please leave," she said politely. She was scaring him.

He sat down beside her on the bed and pulled her hand into his.

"You're not a burden," he said quietly. "I've never seen you as a burden."

"Then you're stupid."

He winced. Aliana had never said that, not ever. She looked up at him and bit her lip.

"I'm sorry Hunter, I didn't mean it."

"Then say what you mean."

"You should go on with your life, I'm nothing more than an anchor. You're getting what you've always wanted. I'm your past."

"You're not my past, you're right in front of me."

"You're a SEAL now. It's what you wanted. I'm letting you go so you can be happy." Her voice trembled on the last word.

"Cut the shit, Alia. I am happy. Being your friend makes me happy."

"I thought so. But I know better now." She started to shut her Bible, but the yellow caught his eye.

"That's the sunflower. Why were you looking at it? I mean something to you? Don't I? If I do, why are you throwing me away?"

"I'm not Hunter," she wailed softly. "I'm saving you. You have to go now."

"Not until you make me understand."

She gave the harshest laugh he'd ever heard. It sounded like something out of a horror movie.

"You never want to understand this, Hunter. It's too ugly. I'm too ugly. I'm a burden. Having me around will cause you to die."

"That's bullshit. Where did you hear that bullshit? Are those bitches at school feeding you some kind of line again? What have they said?"

She got up on her knees and hurled her Bible against the wall. He watched as the dried sunflower and his letter fluttered to the ground.

"Get out! I want you gone. We're done."

The light turned on, and it was Mrs. Novak. She saw him and screamed. He jumped out the window. That was the last time he saw Aliana Novak.

He sent her letter after letter for six months. They all came back return to sender. Even he caught a clue after that long.

* * *

"Lottie, what is this? I could barely zip up these jeans, and you know I would never wear a t-shirt like this. What were you thinking?"

"I was thinking you needed to loosen up."

Hunter recognized the husky voice with the Czech accent. He turned the corner and came face-to-face with his past. She was scowling at a curvy Hispanic woman. Aliana's hair was still incredibly long. He watched as she gathered it up and started to pile it on her head.

"Look at her, she's all bruised. I told you she needed your help. The poor baby," his grandmother said in Spanish.

The two women in the hospital room turned to stare at them.

"Do you just collect hot men?" the cute woman asked as she turned to look at Aliana.

Aliana was frozen, her hair falling from her hands, a golden mass shimmering all around her. He saw her mouth open and silently form his name. She took a stuttering step forward, her hand out, as tears welled in her beautiful blue eyes.

He felt a wrenching in his soul, something shook loose, and he smiled as he moved toward her. But then she stepped backward and brought both her fists to her gut and pressed in like she was in pain. She shook her head at him, and he stopped.

"Alia?"

"No. Please, no."

He stopped.

"Who is this?" Aliana's friend asked gently. She could tell how upset Alia was.

A toilet flushed, the door to the bathroom opened and out walked Mrs. Jankovic.

"Hunter, you came."

"*Babička*, what's going on?" Aliana asked hoarsely. It killed Hunter to see how much pain Aliana was in. She looked like she had been run over by a Mac truck, and it was clear his presence was adding to it.

Her friend did what he wanted to, put her arm around Alia's shoulders and whispered something in her ear. Then she turned to Aliana's grandmother.

"Mrs. Jankovic, who is this?"

"Allow me to introduce." Mrs. Jankovic swept into the middle of the room and kissed his grandmother on the cheek. "Rosa, thank you for bringing your pretty grandson."

She looked up at him. "Bend down. You too tall for me to climb you."

Hunter suppressed a grin. He'd forgotten Mrs. J's ability to butcher the English language. He bent so the noble woman could touch her cheek to his.

"Make this better," she whispered into his ear. "I'm depending on you."

How was he supposed to do that when Aliana was looking at him like he'd killed her puppy? Before he could say anything, Aliana beat him to the punch.

"Lottie, *Babička*, we need to go. It was good seeing you, Mrs. Diaz." She was squeezing his grandmother's hand and giving her a sad, loving smile and totally ignoring him.

"Aliana?"

"I can't, Hunter." She stared at the floor. "I don't feel well, I need to go."

Lottie cleared her throat. "Uhm, Aliana, you need to wait for the wheelchair." Aliana gave her friend a panicked look. "I'm sorry honey, I don't know who he is to you. Maybe he can leave until the doctor gets here."

"No, he's not leaving," her grandmother decreed. "Carlotta, this is Mrs. Diaz and her grandson Hunter Diaz. He's a sailor."

"SEAL," his grandmother corrected.

"But that sounds like a cute little creature of marine life. Sailor sounds more like a man," Mrs. Jankovic said.

Hunter closed his eyes, praying for patience.

"Holy hell, you have a Navy SEAL on tap? No wonder you didn't tell the cops anything," Lottie tried to tease Aliana.

"Please, Lottie, it's not funny." She turned to Hunter. "I don't know what you're doing here, but can you go?"

"He's here to help," her grandmother said.

As much as her anxiety concerned him, one thing bothered him a hell of a lot more.

"Why aren't you cooperating with the police?" Hunter asked Aliana.

She stiffened, then looked down at the floor, "I can't talk about it." She turned and limped toward the bed. "I'm going to phone for the wheelchair."

"You are dirtying this up," Mrs. Jankovic hissed softly at him so that Aliana couldn't hear.

"I'll take care of it," he smiled.

"Good."

She watched the two of them as she made the phone call. "What are you talking about?" she asked as she hung up the phone.

"Aliana, your grandmother called my grandmother. I came to help you."

She bit her lip, then hissed, and brought her hand up to her already swollen mouth.

"Please Alia, let me help you."

She opened her mouth to ask a question, then looked around at the audience they had and shut her mouth. In three steps he was in front of her.

"What?" he asked.

Her pretty face had a unique expression on it. "You're not supposed to be here. You were supposed to stay away."

"I stayed away far too long." Now that he was here, he was thinking he should have been here a damn sight sooner. He realized the look on her face was hope. He knew it as he watched it slip away.

"No, you should never have come back. It's for your own good."

There was a knock behind him.

"Somebody call for a ride?" an orderly with a wheelchair asked.

"That's for me," Aliana said. He walked with her as she gingerly sat down in the chair.

Mrs. Jankovic patted his arm. She leaned in to say something to his grandmother that he couldn't quite make out. Then she and Lottie followed Aliana out of the room.

"*Mamie?*"

"We'll talk about it in the car. Let's give them a chance to go out first. You're upsetting your Alia," she said in Spanish.

"She hasn't been mine for a long time."

"She's always been yours. And she needs you now."

Maybe. He thought about that first moment when she had seen him. Despite everything, her instinct had been to come to him. It was like the clouds parted for just a moment and the sun burst through, shining directly on him. He savored it. But now, he needed to focus on matters at hand.

"Do you know what's going on?"

"I have our book club looking into things."

He stepped back so he could look down at the small woman he called grandmother.

"I did not just hear you say that your book club is trying to figure out who planted a bomb in Aliana's house."

"The twelve of us are very well-connected here in the neighborhood. We're meeting on Saturday. Velma is bringing German chocolate cake, and her aunt is bringing apple pie. I'll have ice cream. We want to bring you up to speed."

"I don't want you involved," he commanded.

"Too late, we're involved. You're coming and listening. I had Velma bake your favorite cake. Don't give me any shit, boy."

Hunter burst out laughing. He hadn't actually been up to visit his grandmother in over a year, and they hadn't argued like this in forever. It was fun. He wrapped her up in a hug.

"I love you *Mamie*, but I'm not letting you and your crazy cronies get involved with street gangs."

"Some of those women were in the original gangs back in the day. They know what's up. Granted, anyone truly loyal to that way of life has long since dropped out of the book club."

He looked down at her. "You're not hearing me. I'm serious, you're not involved. Today you're going to give me the information I need, then you're taking down your Miss Marple Detective Agency shingle. Tell me what I need to know."

"We'll tell you on Saturday."

"I want to know why Aliana hasn't talked to the cops."

Rosa brightened. "She's better now, you know."

"What do you mean better?"

"After her father killed himself, she went into a shell. But it wasn't until six months later that she seemed to disappear."

Six months later would have been when he stopped sending letters. "What do you mean, disappear?"

"It was the beginning of her senior year. Her mother and her grandmother didn't notice."

The back of his neck tingled. "Go on."

"She fainted in school."

"What was wrong with her?"

"She hadn't been eating. She'd lost weight, but she was wearing so many layers of clothes, nobody noticed. They had to hospitalize her."

"Ah shit, *Mamie*."

"According to Magda, it just made her more of a target at school. But there is good news, *mi hijo*, she won a big poetry award and got a scholarship. She got to go to Arizona I think. Anyway, she got out. She came back because her mom got sick. She's a good girl. She takes care of her mama."

"Her mom's sick?"

"Alzheimer's. Aliana had to eventually put her in a home. For a long time, though, she was living with Aliana, but now that she is a vice principal, she can afford a place."

"She's a vice principal?"

"Yes, at Bertrum High School."

His Alia had come a long way. But then he thought about her having to take care of a mother who was slowly losing herself and his heart ached all over again for her.

"Why isn't she talking to the cops?" he asked.

"This is the first I heard about it. You need to find out. In the meantime, I'll tell the girls in the club about the latest developments."

Holy hell. "*Mamie,* stop with the book club already. I'm going to take care of everything. What gang is after her? Is it *Las Nuevas Espadas?*"

"Velma doesn't think so. She'll know more on Saturday when you get your cake."

God, there was no stopping his grandmother.

CHAPTER FOUR

"She doesn't want to see you."

"You need an alarm system. You didn't even turn on the porch light," Hunter chided the older lady.

"You have screwed the cat. Aliana is resting. Seeing you upset her. You here will make her more so. I cannot let you in." He saw she was leaning heavily on the doorjamb. He hated seeing the strong woman looking so frail.

"*Babička*, who's at the—?" She was smiling until she saw him, then she shut down. "Hi, Hunter, what are you doing here?" He winced at the bruising on the side of her face and arm and the bandage on her neck.

He couldn't very well throw Mrs. J under the bus and say she invited him. "I wanted to know about your conversations with the police."

"Yes, what about them?" her grandmother asked, looking up at her.

Aliana threw Hunter a frustrated look.

"I'm taking care of everything," she told both of them.

"Hunter can take care of everything, you're tired. The doctor said you still need more rest, Láska. He doesn't want you to go out of the house until Friday."

"I'm fine, *Babička*," she stroked her grandmother's shoulder. "Why don't you go inside and sit down. I'll just have a few words with Hunter before he leaves, okay?"

Mrs. Jankovic frowned. "We should invite him in. I made Marlenka honey cake," she said stubbornly. He had to admire the woman for sticking to a plan, but he hated how Aliana looked like a trapped kitten. She didn't know if she should run or try out her sharp little claws.

"That sounds wonderful, Mrs. J."

"I'll go get it," her grandmother said. She was clearly relieved that he had gone along with her efforts.

Aliana smiled at her grandmother. "I'll serve it. You go to the parlor, I'll bring it out to both of you." As soon as her grandmother turned around, Aliana fixed him with a fierce stare. Apparently, she was going with the kitten claws.

He laughed. "I'm going to help Alia," he called out to the older woman as she slowly started to make her way to another room.

"You're such a gentleman," Mrs. Jancovik called out over her shoulder.

He followed Aliana into the kitchen. "So, tell me why you haven't been forthcoming with the police."

She stopped in the middle of the kitchen and spun around. She lost her balance, it was clear she wasn't used to being injured. He put his hand under her elbow to brace her.

"Careful, *mi Cariña*, you just got out of the hospital."

"I would take better care of myself if you weren't making me so confused," she said weakly.

He guided her towards the kitchen table and had them both sitting down.

"Just think of me like the tide. I'm here to stay and there's nothing you can do to stop me, so you might as well just go with the flow."

She pushed her hair out of her face and grimaced as she touched the bruise at her temple. "But that's the thing, I don't want you here."

He winced.

She reached over and touched his hand. Stroked it.

"Please don't make me beg you. You don't belong here anymore. You have a life apart from mine. Please live it, for your own sake, I want what's best for you. I have my mom to take care of, I have a life with *Babička* and my job. Hunter, my problems are no longer your problems, okay?"

It hurt. Even after thirteen years being told she didn't want him in her life still felt like a punch in the gut. It would have hurt a hell of a lot more if he hadn't smelled the bullshit. She wanted him here as much as he needed to be here. Nobody giving someone a brush off would basically hold their hand. He'd had brush-offs, and they didn't work that way.

But there was something going on. There was part of her that wanted him gone. Was it their past history together? Was it whatever trouble which had her in its sights? He didn't know, but he intended to find out. He put his hand over hers.

"You're avoiding the question, Alia. What *haven't* you told the cops?"

She looked away and pushed up from the table. "I'll get the cake."

"Answer the question."

Aliana went to the counter and lifted the lid off a cake stand. She slowly pulled out a knife from the butcher block and ran her finger along the side of it. Then she turned to him.

"I'll tell you what I told them," she said very calmly. "Somebody I didn't know saw fit to plant a bomb in my home. I've made some enemies at school. Kids have threatened me when I've suspended or expelled them. It could have been any one of them. I gave them some names." She set the knife down beside the cake and pulled three plates out of the cupboard.

"But you don't think it was one of them, do you?" he asked slowly.

"It could be," she hedged as she picked up a plate to put a slice of cake on it.

It was a bunch of crap.

"You do realize you're putting your grandmother at risk by not cooperating, don't you?"

The dish she had been holding clattered to the counter, but didn't break. She looked up at him, her face a sick shade of white.

"Fuck, you hadn't thought of that." She shook her head. "Why not?"

"Nobody mentioned her, and we have different last names. I'm such an idiot. *Sakra!* Fuck!" Her eyes filled with tears.

"Hey, hey, hey. You're not an idiot," he said. He tried to pull her away from the counter.

"I've got to finish, *Babička* is waiting for us."

"She can wait a little longer. Tell me who the people were who didn't mention your grandmother. Somebody threatened your mother?"

She shook her head, refusing to look at him.

"*Cariña*, you've got to tell me."

She pulled away from him and her gaze swung wildly around the kitchen. "I can fix this. I can fix this." She mutters.

"No you can't, not without my help."

"Dammit, Hunter. I told you to go away. You listened before why not this time?" She looked at him beseechingly.

"Because now I'm thirty-one, not a dumb nineteen-year-old who had my teeth kicked in by the girl who meant everything to him. This time we're going to resolve this shit. You're going to let me help, and you're going to tell me why you sent me away all those years ago."

"Please, leave, I'm begging you. It's what's best." More tears spilled. She looked wildly around the kitchen. He followed her glance. Her eyes spied the knife. For a second he thought she was going to grab it, but then she turned to face him.

"Best for who? It's sure as hell not best for me."

"Then me. Leave so I can still feel good about myself." She stared past him at the counter. "When I told you to go away before, I was relieving you of a responsibility that would just make you have a crap life." Her head swung so she could glare at him. "But it got even worse Hunter, far worse. You were so lucky you got away from the crazy girl when you did."

"What in the world are you talking about. *Mamie* can't sing your praises enough. Your grandmother adores you. You're a Vice Principal, for God's sake."

"Are you going to go?" she asked, her voice a hoarse whisper.

He gently placed his hands on her shoulders, not in a million years did he want to cause her physical pain on her bruises.

"Nothing is going to drag me away."

She closed her eyes and sucked in a deep breath. Then blew out a breath. She did it rhythmically. He recognized the pattern, he'd done it at his friend's dojo, and also when he was on the rifle range. Finally, she opened her eyes.

"Fine. Just fine."

"Are you going to tell me why you told me to leave thirteen years ago?"

She shook her head.

He nodded, unsurprised.

"We really need to get the cake out to *Babička*."

"Not before you tell me what you haven't told the police."

"I told them that I expelled some gang members last month, and it must be retaliation for that."

He stared at her. He found that pretty fucking hard to believe. Not the fact that she'd told the police the bullshit story, but that was what had caused her home to blow up. He looked at her and saw the telltale blush creeping up her neck.

"You want to pull the other leg?"

She stood up straighter. "What are you talking about?" she asked indignantly. "That is exactly what I told the police."

"I don't doubt that, but it's hardly the full truth. Now, what the hell are you hiding, Alia?"

She just stared at him, her blue eyes shooting fire.

Fuck, he wasn't going to win. He started to laugh.

She put her hands on her hips. "Why are you laughing?"

"Because I'm screwed."

"Join the club. I've asked you to leave, and you're being stubborn and staying. You're annoying the hell out of me."

"Come on, Alia, admit this is a little fun. You used to laugh." The blue fire turned into a bit of a sparkle.

"I admit nothing."

"I can't even get a smile out of you?"

"Can you not back off?" she asked with exasperation.

"Nope, did that thirteen years ago. I'm planted this time. How about that smile?"

Her lip quirked up at the corner.

"God, you've turned into a beautiful woman."

"Don't say that. I don't need your lies."

Her sparkle left. He stared at her dumbfounded. She was serious. He took his hands away from her cheeks, and she let go of him. Then he stroked his knuckles down her arms.

"I wouldn't lie to you about this or be glib. We've been through too much real shit together. I've been in the trenches with you, Alia. You were always pretty, and your hair was gorgeous, that's why those bitches were always pulling at it. But now, especially when you light up and smile, you're beautiful."

"I don't understand you, Hunter."

"I see that," he pushed back a strand of hair behind her ear. "Give it time. Let's get your grandma her cake."

* * *

Aliana's cell phone rang, it was the school and she had to take it. That left Hunter staring at Mrs. Jankovic.

"She doesn't look upset. You did good." The old woman looked pleased. "How are you going to fix things for my granddaughter?"

He liked this woman a lot. No wonder she was friends with his *Mamie*.

"I thought we might finish the cake before we got into the third degree."

"Third degree?"

"Interrogation," he explained as he took another bite of cake.

"Do you like it?"

"It's fantastic. What kind is it again?"

"Marlenka honey cake. It is my mother's recipe from the old country. Now, how are you going to make things better?"

He considered what to tell her.

"I'm going to call in a friend of mine," he started.

"Phhhft. Not that. How are you going to fix it with her emotions?"

"What?" What was she talking about?

"My Aliana has been locked up into herself for many years. She has never worked past what happened the year her father died and you left. Were you her boyfriend?"

He set down his empty plate and gave her his full attention.

"She was my best friend in the world."

"What were you doing in her bedroom that night?"

"At your son-in-law's wake, she told me she never wanted to see me again. I had to understand why, so I went to see her."

The old women peered deeply into his eyes. "I believe you. Now tell me what you are going to do to make her happy."

"I'm still trying to get a handle on that."

"A handle?" she asked.

"I'm still trying to figure it out."

She grabbed both of his big hands in her frail ones. "Well, let us figure it out together."

"I can't right now, I have to go out and keep watch."

"What do you mean?"

"Mrs. J. since someone blew up Aliana's house, I'm worried about both of your safety. I want somebody watching your house at all times."

"But you can't do that. You need to sleep."

"I'll have a friend who will be here tonight to take over."

"Who?"

"His name is Dalton Sullivan. He's a SEAL too. He's on my team."

"A sailor?"

"Yes, a sailor," he sighed.

"Strong like you?"

"Yes."

"Big like you?"

Hunter paused.

Mrs. Jankovic laughed. "Nobody is as big as you are."

Hunter thought about Drake Avery and Zed Zaragoza. "I know two who are the same size," he said wryly. "But I don't think they're available." But maybe…

She let go of his hands and patted his arm. "I like sailors. You're good boys. Aliana will see that. You come back tomorrow. I'll make breakfast."

He got up, picked up his dish, and held out his hand to take hers back to the kitchen. She stood up as well.

"Now bend down." She kissed his cheek. "You protect us. Find these ugly guys. I want my granddaughter safe."

"I promise."

He left her house and went across the street to *Mamie's* car. It was a beige Buick that didn't look out of place in the neighborhood. But him sitting in it for hours on end would. That was fine with him. He wanted to put people on notice that these women were being watched over. He pulled out his phone and called Zed first.

"It's been a long time. Why the late call?" Zed asked.

"I'm taking a chance. I'm basically on top of the El Monte busway, close to the 60 Freeway."

"What the fuck are you doing there at this time of night? That's not where your grandmother lives." Zed was pissed.

"An old friend has a problem."

"I don't care. Get your ass back to Coronado. Unless you're visiting your grandmother, you stay out of gang territory. I told you that sixteen years ago. That life has to be dead to you."

Now Hunter was pissed. Zed might be second-in-command of his unit. He might have been the one who put him on the straight and narrow all those years ago, but he sure as hell didn't need him talking to him like he was some sort of dimwitted child.

"Zed, I called you for a reason. If you're going to be an asshole, I'll hang up."

The silence was so long, Hunter looked down at his phone to see if his friend had hung up. Nope, they were still connected.

"Just got back from a bad one four days ago. Lost a man."

Hunter was stunned. A SEAL dead, and he hadn't heard about it? "Did I know him?"

"He was our liaison. Didn't pay attention to orders. Still doesn't matter, it was on my watch." It wouldn't matter. Hunter might never have served with Dante 'Zed' Zaragoza, but he knew what kind of man, what kind of second-in-command he was. He would see this as a personal failure.

"What's next for you?"

"We just spent a shit ton of time doing debriefs. We've got downtime, and it's been suggested, strongly, that I take some leave. Apparently, they think I'm close to the edge."

"Are you?"

"No." Another long pause. "Yeah, maybe a little. I feel guilty, but you suck it up. This is part of the job. If I thought I couldn't lead men into battle and handle the consequences, I'd hang up my boots."

Hunter smiled. Now that was the man he knew. "But it would make command happy if you took leave?"

"What do you have in mind? Because as much as I suggested you stay out of the 'hood, same goes for me."

"I have an old friend. Went to school with her. She was two years younger than me, and—"

"Aliana Novak," Zed interrupted. "I looked her up when I approached you. I investigated everything about you, Kid."

Hunter hadn't been called a kid, well, except for Zed, he'd never been called a kid.

"Anyway, she's the Vice Principal of Bertrum High School, and her house just got blown up. By sheer luck, she didn't die."

"Who's targeting her?"

"One of the local gangs. I've got to find out which one, but she needs protection. I'm calling in a friend from Black Dawn. We're between missions, so Gray should give him leave. But it would be really helpful to have another set of eyes who know their way around here."

"She's a Vice Principal? Who would have guessed it?"

"Not me. But she doesn't want me here."

"But you're staying, anyway?"

"What do you think?"

Zed chuckled. "Let me straighten some things out. I'll be there day after tomorrow."

"Sounds good," Hunter said, hanging up the phone.

Hunter saw a dark Charger coming down the street, driving very slowly. He got out of his car and leaned against the driver's side door, his arms crossed over his massive chest, waiting to see who was driving. The car was matte black, and he saw two young Hispanic men in the front seat and two in the back. He stared at them. They slowed down even more, the stupid fucks. The passenger put a Smith and Wesson .38 on the dashboard for him to see. He pushed back one side of his windbreaker and gave them a glance of his Sig Sauer pistol. They stopped the car. Even dumber. Who knew, he might be giving his body armor a work out after all. He walked up to the car and waited for them to speak. It didn't take long for them to break the silence.

"You don't belong here," the driver said belligerently.

Hunter just stared at them. They were young, not even twenty.

"Did you hear me? I said pack it up."

Hunter still didn't respond. The driver turned to his three friends. "Dummy can't even speak," he said in Spanish. "The bitch has got herself a retard to guard her."

Everyone in the car started laughing. The driver casually reached for the .38 on the dashboard. Hunter waited, knowing what was next. The driver turned his wrist sideways.

"Do you see what I have for you? Do you?" He jabbed the gun into Hunter's belly, hitting his body armor. It took a split second for Hunter to disarm him and shove the gun into the young man's skull.

"Don't call those ladies bitches. Understand?" he said in Spanish. He gave a quick glance to the two in the backseat and laughed. "Don't make a move for your little pea-shooters. Really, you're both sporting .22s?"

Neither one of them looked old enough to shave. Both slunk down in their seats. The one in the passenger seat, tattoos crawling up his neck, glared at Hunter.

"What do you want?" the driver asked, a hint of a stutter in his voice.

"It's not what I want. I was just standing here minding my own business, when you four ass-clowns show up, deciding to wave your pieces. Why are you here?"

"No reason."

Hunter dug the tip of the pistol into the guy's flesh, hard, and he hissed out a breath.

"I can do this all day. As a matter of fact, it's breaking up the monotony." Hunter twisted the gun so that the tip dug deeper. This time, the man let out a squeak of pain.

"Mateo told us to see if the bitch's granddaughter was here," the driver said.

That was good, they weren't sure Aliana was here, but who was Mateo?

"You *Las Nuevas Espadas*?" Hunter asked.

A series of 'No' and 'Fuck No', resounded through the car.

"Those guys are pussies," the driver said.

"You need to come up with a new insult," Hunter admonished. "So you're *Los Demonios*?"

"Goddamn right, we are," the one in the in the passenger seat said. He pulled down his wife-beater tank and pointed proudly at a tattoo of some kind Halloween figure. Hunter figured it was supposed to be a demon. "See. We're *Los Demonios*," he said proudly.

"What do the *Los Demonios* want with Mrs. Jankovic's granddaughter?" Hunter asked.

"She's messing with our family," the driver said. "Mateo is pissed. She's causing trouble, stirring things up."

"How?"

"I don't know."

Hunter looked at tattoo boy. "How?"

"It's above my rank. We're just supposed to check to see if she's here. Just Mateo, the other lieutenants, and San Marcos really know what's going on. We only heard the rumors."

"Let me get this straight. The leader of the gang called the Demons is St. Mark?"

"Pretty cool, huh?" The tattoo guy smiled. Hunter shook his head. To think he used to be a part of this madness.

Out of the corner of his eye, he saw one of the kids in the back fumble with his gun. Hunter, gripped the driver with his left hand by the throat, easily cutting off his air, then aimed his gun at the teen in the back.

"Do you want to die today? Are you straight with God? Been to mass recently? What's your Mama going to say?"

The kid blanched.

"Put the gun on the floor." He motioned to the other kid. "You too." He kept an eye on tattoo boy as well. The driver was trying to break his hold, but it was impossible. He was thrashing and turning purple. "Better hurry before your friend runs out of air."

"You won't kill him."

"Won't be the first time I killed somebody, not by a long shot. Won't be the last."

"Who the fuck are you?" tattoo boy asked.

"I'm a friend of Mrs. Jankovic. I'm also a friend of her granddaughter. I don't give a shit if she's messing with your family. I consider them *my* family. Got it?"

The guns were put on the floor of the car. He released the unconscious driver who slumped onto the steering wheel.

"Guess you'll be driving," he said to the guy in the passenger seat. "I want you gone. Tell this guy Mateo to leave these women alone."

Tattoo boy laughed. "You don't know who you're dealing with."

"No, he doesn't know who *he's* dealing with," Hunter chuckled. "Just pass the message along. Now you two ass-clowns, pick up your guns by the muzzle and hand them to me."

"But—"

"Do it," the guy in the front seat said.

Hunter collected the two small caliber guns, then backed away from the car. He watched as the tattooed guy got out of the car and went to the driver's side so he could take over driving.

"Mateo is going to be pissed," he said as he passed Hunter.

"Tell Mateo I'm already pissed, so we're even. Now get the fuck out of here."

He watched as the car took off down the street at a much faster speed than when it arrived. Damn, the license plates were missing.

Yep, he definitely needed backup.

He put the three extra guns in the trunk of his grandmother's Buick. Sitting in the car, he pulled out his phone.

Dalton was number one on his speed dial. They'd been through BUD/S together, but hadn't ended up on the same team. Hunter was lucky, he'd always been on Black Dawn, Dalton had been assigned to a team which had eventually disbanded. Though they hadn't been on the same missions together, they'd remained close, even during that miserable final year Dalton spent with Cindy. And the tragic ending that ripped at Hunter's guts whenever he thought about it.

He blew out a breath through clenched teeth and whispered a quick prayer up to heaven. Then he called Dalton.

"Hey. Wondered when you'd call."

"Now. I'm calling now."

Dalton chuckled. "Whatcha need?"

Hunter loved that. No question in his mind, he was going to help Hunter out.

"Did Gray say anything?" Hunter asked.

"You're kidding, right? Our lieutenant reveal any personal information? Hell, we could waterboard him, and he still wouldn't tell anyone your favorite fingernail polish. You still like to wear hot pink, right?"

Hunter appreciated Dalton's teasing. The man knew something was up and was trying to make him relax.

"Fuchsia. They call it fuchsia. We need to work on your metro-sexualness."

"So, what's up, Diaz?"

"I'm up in East L.A. Gang territory. There's a new gang who has its sights set on an old friend."

"Aliana?"

Hunter didn't know how to respond.

"You talked a lot about her in BUD/S. I can't imagine anyone other than your grandmother who would have you going back home."

"Yeah, it's her. They blew up her townhome last night. She's lucky she escaped with her life." Hunter heard a cabinet closing over the phone.

"How soon do you need me there?"

"How soon can you get here?"

"Just give me the address, I'm already packing."

"*Mamie* has a washing machine you can use," Hunter grinned.

* * *

Hunter was beginning to get a feel for the neighborhood. It was a good, hard-working, poor community who looked after one another. He'd been approached four times by concerned citizens, usually in groups. But one older lady, who reminded him of *Mamie*, came bearing a cup of coffee. When he saw her approach, he got out of his car.

"Magda told me what you're doing. She goes to bed early, but wanted me to make sure you stayed alert."

"Thank you, ma'am. That's awfully thoughtful of you."

He took a sip of the coffee and hid his grimace. This wasn't coffee, it was ground up coffee beans mixed with a tablespoon of water. He'd never tasted such sludge.

"This isn't to my taste, but she said you were a sailor and would like it really thick. I brought you some brownies too." She handed him a Tupperware container. "Do you want me to come and top you off later?"

"I'm good," he choked out.

"How about some milk to go with the brownies? Magda didn't say anything about sailors liking milk, but my husband likes milk when he eats my brownies."

God, yes. Anything to get rid of the taste in his mouth.

"That would be very nice, Ma'am."

"Call me Beatrice."

"Thank you, Beatrice." He continued to look around her so he could keep watch of the Jankovic house.

"I'll be back." She gave a small wave. When he saw another car approaching, he leaned into the Buick and grabbed his water bottle and took a quick drink. The police car pulled in behind him, but its lights didn't come on. The officer got out of the car and came over to him.

"Are you Ernie?" Hunter asked.

"Lottie called me. I assume you're Hunter Diaz?" Hunter nodded. "Got some I.D.?"

Hunter pulled out his wallet and showed him his driver's license, military I.D. card, and Concealed Weapons Permit.

"Good to meet you." Ernie held out his hand.

Hunter stared at it. Ernie scowled. "What's with the attitude?"

"Why haven't I seen any cops driving by tonight? You're the first one in five hours."

"What are you talking about, there should have been at least one an hour?"

"There hasn't been."

"Hold on, let me check on this." He walked briskly back to his car. He was obviously pissed, which made Hunter happy. Then he spied Beatrice. She had his milk.

"Is something wrong? Is he harassing you? I can go talk to him if you need me to."

Hunter took the glass of milk and drank down half of it, then swiped his mouth.

"No, he's a friend." The last thing he needed was Beatrice going to bat for him with the cop. How had he ended up with a Lady's Brigade rushing to defend, feed, and investigate things? *Mamie*, sure, but the rest of them? It was getting kind of spooky. Wait until Zed and Dalton ran up against them.

"You don't look sure," she interrupted his musings. "I'm part of the neighborhood watch. I have a badge and everything. Let me go speak with him."

Hunter put a hand on her shoulder. "Seriously, he's a good guy. He's looking over Mrs. Jankovic and Aliana too."

"Really? Well, he's not doing a good job of it." Ernie was walking back. "Shouldn't you have been here sooner?" Beatrice asked the man. "If you're watching out for my neighbor, you should do a better job."

Ernie gave Hunter a questioning look. "I told her that you were here to help."

"And your name is?" Ernie asked the woman.

"Beatrice Price. I live over there," she said, indicating the pea green house. "I'm the president of the neighborhood watch. With what happened to poor Aliana, I would have thought there would have been more of a police presence."

"You're absolutely right, ma'am." Ernie looked chagrined. "There was a mistake on the address. From now on there will be a patrol car coming by at least every hour if not more often."

"That's good." She turned to Hunter. "But you're staying?"

"Yes, until my friend arrives."

"He is in the Army too?"

"Navy. We're both in the Navy." He saw Ernie smirk out of the corner of his eye. Apparently, he had looked up his record.

"Have you ever fought? Because these bastards used a bomb. Aliana needs strong protection."

"Yes, ma'am, I've fought. So has my friend. We know what we're doing."

"I'm trusting you."

"I appreciate that, and I won't let you down." It took everything he had not to chuckle. He needed to treat her concerns with the utmost respect, but for real?

"I'll be watching you. As long as you do a good job, I'll bring you coffee and treats."

"What about me?" Ernie asked.

"You screwed up. You didn't earn it." With that, she turned and left.

"Be happy, the coffee is godawful," Hunter said with a grin as soon as she was out of earshot.

"She's a hoot."

"God save me from little old ladies."

"What do you mean?" Ernie asked.

"I mean that I have my grandmother's book club planning to get information on who is after Aliana."

"What?" Ernie looked incredulous. "Did you say grandmother?"

"Not just *Mamie*, but her book club. I think there are ten of them. I've been invited to a meeting, they're serving German chocolate cake. The hell of it is, I think they might have some useful info."

"No way. They need to stay the fuck out of this," Ernie said vehemently.

"I'll try to dissuade them."

"Invite me. I'll get the point across."

"I'm with Beatrice, you screwed up, you didn't earn it."

"Watch it. I'm the cop in this neighborhood, don't think you can come in here and run roughshod over this investigation. You're out of line."

"Well, you're doing a shitty job."

"Really? Have you gotten her to tell you who assaulted her last week? Because if you did that would sure help us figure out who planted the bomb yesterday."

"Assault? What assault?"

"Her throat and chest were cut. She required stitches."

Shit, he'd seen the bandage on her throat and just assumed it was from the bomb.

"When did this happen?"

"Friday. She reluctantly ID'd the car, but she wouldn't say who cut her. I'm positive she knew who did it." Ernie rolled back and forth on his feet, clearly frustrated.

"Does the name Mateo mean anything to you?"

"No. Should it?"

"I had a run in with some members of *Los Demonios* a little earlier. They drove a 2015 Charger, matte black. There were no plates on the car. They said Mateo had a special interest in Aliana. I think he's a lieutenant."

"Well the car doesn't match the one she ID'd on Saturday," Ernie sighed. "Like I said, never heard the name, but I can check with the gang and narcotics division."

"Do that."

"Yes, Sir," Ernie said sarcastically.

"Look, asshole, we're on the same team." Hunter didn't need a territorial pissing match, not when Aliana's life was on the line.

Ernie leaned in—he was only an inch shorter than Hunter, probably not used to dealing with anyone bigger than himself—and he was angry.

"We have detectives who are on top of this."

"I'm the one who's going to get Aliana to talk. I'm the one who can devote people 24/7 to making sure she and her grandmother are safe. I'm the one who can make sure these fucks back off for good."

"You do something illegal, and I'll be forced to put you away."

"I won't do anything that will get me put away." Hell, if he couldn't handle staying out of the frying pan, he didn't deserve to be called a SEAL.

Ernie gave him an assessing look. "I heard what you didn't say. I don't like it."

"Sue me."

"I'm going to have my eye on you."

"Why don't you be on the lookout for the bastards who are after Aliana. Wouldn't that be a better use of your time?"

"I can multi-task."

"Since you're so great at multi-tasking, why don't you see what you can do with these." Hunter popped the trunk of his car and pulled out the three guns he'd confiscated.

"What the fuck?"

"I'm giving you a gift," Hunter said with a wry smile. "*Los Demonios* were kind enough to give up their weapons to me."

"Kind? You guys have a tea party?"

"Something like that."

Ernie carefully took the wrapped guns from Hunter.

"Hopefully you can get some usable prints."

"Why, are you going to file a complaint against them? Seems to me if they were so *kind*, they might want to file charges against you."

"Aliana might want to file a complaint."

"Yeah, sure," Ernie said derisively. "I'll hold my breath."

"So the patrols are going to be more frequent?"

"Yep, and not just because of *Los Demonios*. Seems to me, we need to keep an eye on you."

"Yeah, I got that." Geez, couldn't the guy go already?

"You staying here tonight?"

"Until a friend of mine shows up. Then I'm going to take a little break."

"What should I tell the patrol to be on the lookout for?"

Please God, say Dalton wouldn't be driving his Corvette. "A beat-up, rusted, baby blue, 1990 Chevy truck."

Ernie wrote it down in his notebook, "I take it being a SEAL doesn't pay well?"

"Nope."

"I'll see you around."

Not if he saw him first. Hunter got back into his grandmother's car and watched Ernie pull away from the curb. Now he just had to wait for Dalton to show up.

* * *

Hunter heard the truck before he saw it. It might look like a piece of shit, but Dalton had put in a cat-back exhaust system and a supercharger. The damn thing was hell on wheels. The only thing that made people realize there was more than meets the eye to the truck were the high-performance tires. Hunter got out of his car, confident in the knowledge Dalton would spot him in the dark. His friend found the one open parking spot on the street half a block back. Hunter watched Dalton's tall, sleekly muscled frame prowl towards him.

"Nice car. Not as nice as my truck, but nice," Dalton said, nodding at the Buick.

"Don't be making fun of my Mamie's car, you *bastardo*."

Dalton chuckled. "So, what's the scoop with Aliana. Is she finally speaking to you?" he asked kindly.

"Hell, Dalton, I'm not sure, but I think I'm making some headway, but it's definitely going to be an uphill climb."

"Well, at least it's you and not me. You have the ability to play all the angles."

"You used to," Hunter reminded his friend.

"That was a century ago, I'm not that man anymore. What you see is what you get." God, he hoped not. Dalton hadn't been truly happy in years. "Hunter, we're not about to have a heart to heart in the middle of the street when we're supposed to be guarding your high school sweetheart and her grandmother, are we?"

"Huh? What are you talking about? Aliana was never my girlfriend. She was just a friend." He remembered the last time he had seen Aliana when she'd been sixteen. The moon bathing her face in through her bedroom window as she yelled at him. Even then, there was the hint of the beauty she was going to become.

"Come on Hunter, admit it. You talked about her all the time the first year we served. Then after her father died, I remember what a wreck you were each time you got back an unopened letter."

Dalton was right, he had been.

"You've got it all wrong. I never saw her like that."

"Fine, she wasn't your girlfriend. What is she now? Or better yet, what could she be?"

"Damn, man, today was the first time I saw her in thirteen years. You must think I work as fast as Wyatt."

"I'm not talking about bedding somebody. I'm talking about leading with your heart. I'm saying you were gone over this girl thirteen years ago. I'm saying you swore you were never coming back here except for short little visits to your grandmother, and here you are in the middle of gang business for this woman. I'd say you're leading with your heart, not your head."

"So, you are comparing me to Wyatt," Hunter said.

"Fuck no, he leads with his dick."

Hunter snorted. It was so true. That boy needed a couple more years of seasoning.

"Okay, Dalton, I don't know where I stand with Alia. All I know is I can't handle leaving it where it is now."

"Where is it?"

"I thought we weren't going to have a heart to heart out in the middle of the street?"

"Oh, now that we're not dredging up my shit, I'm fine," Dalton grinned.

Hunter shook his head. God, he loved this man. "Get your ass into your truck. I'm going to do a little reconnaissance."

"What kind?" Dalton asked all business.

"Just a quick little jaunt around the old neighborhood."

"I see you're armored up and loaded for bear," Dalton said, pointing to Hunter's holstered gun and body armor. "I'm betting there's probably more to it than a little walkabout."

"You'd win that bet. A car full of gang members showed up about three hours ago. They were small-time. It took me about a minute to disarm them. I highly doubt they'll be back. They were here to determine if Alia was staying at her grandmother's house. Then there's a patrolman who has a hard-on for Alia, who stopped by to check on her. He gave me a bit of a hassle. I gave him the guns I confiscated from the baby gangbangers."

Dalton chuckled, "So, is the cop competition?"

"Doubt it. Alia basically has the Great Wall of China built up around her. I can't imagine anyone getting through."

"Except you."

"I don't know, Dalton."

"Have faith, Brother. What are you hoping to find when you tour your old haunts?"

"Information about somebody named Mateo. Apparently, he has it out for Aliana. Also turns out besides having her townhome blown to smithereens, she was cut up during an assault last week. She needed stitches. She failed to mention that."

"Down boy."

"Trying to get any information out of her is like pulling teeth."

"Well, won't it be nice to know that your woman won't be talking out of turn?"

"Jesus, what is with you?" Hunter stared at Dalton who just grinned wider.

"Hunter, you're not seeing the forest for the trees. But I'm going to my truck now."

"I'll be back to spell you in a couple of hours."

"No need. I napped today, I knew you'd be calling. I'm good. Go get some shut-eye after you're done doing your recon. You need to figure out how to break down the Great Wall of China." Dalton started whistling 'The Way We Were' as he walked down the street. He had clearly lost his damn mind.

CHAPTER FIVE

Hunter knew exactly where he was going. He drove a mile south of *Las Nuevas Espada's* territory. Hell, now he was in the middle of Crip's turf. He ditched the windbreaker and pulled on a plain gray sweat jacket with a hood. He didn't want to have anything making him stand out more than his size. He kept his head down as he moved silently down the streets, staying in the shadows. Once or twice, he saw someone glance his way, but they decided to leave him alone. Smart move.

Finally, he crossed the busy street that took him to the outskirts of the *Espada's*. He grinned when he walked by Uncle Julio's barbershop. It was the first place he'd ever had his hair cut. *Mamie* had taken him there right before first grade. Before then, someone had always picked up whatever scissors were handy and just chopped away. He looked in the window. There was a light in the back that allowed him to see the barber chairs. He wondered if Julio was still alive. He hoped so, he was an institution in the neighborhood.

Out of the corner of his eye, he saw someone checking him out. When he turned, he realized it was just a prostitute trying to determine if he was a potential client. He shook his head. She walked on down the street. Had they always been that young?

He continued on, walking slowly, wanting to see if he recognized any familiar faces. It's not like he'd be welcomed with open arms, but eventually, he figured there could be a meeting of minds. He came up to the ABC liquor store where Sonny had been killed when he was twelve years old. He'd been stupid enough to go in with his older brother, both of them carrying. Sonny had been in his grade at school. He wasn't even in any of the gangs, nobody wanted him because he was too stupid. That was probably why he ended up dead. Hunter wondered how many of his other friends were now dead, the ones who had been smart enough to be recruited into the gangs, but not smart enough to get out. He crossed another street.

It was two o'clock in the morning, and he would guess the three kids on the upcoming corner couldn't be more than fourteen. Apparently, school wasn't a priority. They looked over at him, and one of them started texting on his phone. Hunter wasn't surprised when an Escalade rolled up two minutes later, and he was surrounded by young, bald, tattooed Chicanos who eyed him up and down.

"Gotta name?" the youngest of the four asked in Spanish. Hunter pegged him to be in his early twenties, the oldest was maybe thirty. He looked at him carefully to see if he recognized him. He didn't.

"Yeah. I gotta name," Hunter said. "Who's asking?"

He was shoved from behind. He'd been expecting it, he didn't budge. Some things never changed. "Tell us your name," the young guy demanded again.

"Is LL still running things?" On his trips up to visit *Mamie*, Hunter had learned his best friend had wrested the leadership from Red Blade.

The oldest guy eyed him up and down. "Just because you know a name, doesn't mean shit. L.A.P.D. sends in people all the goddamn time. Give us a name."

Now he was getting somewhere. No way was he going to talk to anyone but the highest ranking person in this little group.

"Hunter Diaz. LL knows me."

"Well, you better be one hundred percent sure that's true before we give him a call. Otherwise, this conversation ends with you dead. Understood?"

"Just call the man." Hunter was sick of the posturing.

The man whipped out his phone and sent a text. The phone rang in less than a minute. He looked up at Hunter in surprise. "LL wants to talk to you," he said, handing the phone to Hunter.

"That you Hunter? For real?"

"Yep."

"Still a talkative bastard."

"Yep."

"Got to ask you a couple of questions to make sure it's actually you, understand? Need to take precautions."

"Understood." LL had always been smart, that's why he wanted to talk to him.

LL laughed. "If this is you, you're still the same. So, what did you do when you left?"

"Enlisted in the Navy."

"What name did you call your grandmother?"

"*Mamie.*"

"What was the last thing I told you?"

"You'd kill me if I ever showed my face again." Hunter remembered it like it was yesterday. LL had been pretty serious. But then again, LL had been his best friend, and that counted for something. As mad as he was at for Hunter leaving, he respected him too.

"So, asshole, why the fuck did you return?"

"Need a favor."

LL laughed. Kept laughing. Hunter wasn't surprised. Even as a boy, LL always liked a challenge and had a quirky sense of humor.

"Okay, now that we've established you've got the balls of a bull, tell me why I shouldn't have my boys kill you?"

"First, you'd want to do it yourself." Hunter was taking a calculated gamble. But he knew people, and he knew LL.

"Truth." LL was still laughing.

"Second, I can do you a favor."

"I'm listening."

"I'm going to do some damage to *Los Demonios*."

LL started laughing again. "How much damage?"

"They fucked with Aliana. Tried to kill her. They're going to pay. So it's going to be substantial."

"Shit, that's a lot of words. But tell me friend, just you and what army?"

"I've got two friends with me."

"God, man, you've lost your fucking mind. So what favor do you need from me?"

"Intel."

LL sighed. "Give the phone back to Pablo."

Pablo stared darkly at Hunter the entire time he listened to LL. It was clear he wasn't happy with what LL was telling him. He'd wanted to kill Hunter. "Okay, okay. I hear you," he finally said. LL must have hung up because Pablo looked at the others in his group.

"We have to take this guy to LL."

"For real?" the young guy asked.

"Shut up. I tell you something, you do it. No questions. Got it?"

The kid shut up and nodded.

"You," the man said, pointing at Hunter. "You're sitting in the back." He turned to one of the other guys. "Tie him up and blindfold him."

Hunter held out his hands in front of him, and the dumbass tied him that way. Then they tied a scarf around his eyes. Real amateur hour. They shoved him into the backseat of the

SUV. Damn, it even had that new car smell. LL must be doing pretty good for himself. Wonder if the *Los Demonios* had Escalades?

They went eight blocks up and four blocks over. No real need for the wheels and the blindfold had been no use whatsoever, not that he was going to tell them.

Hunter pretended to scratch his head with his shoulder and was able to move his blindfold enough to watch as they pulled up in front of an auto body shop. One of the young men jumped out of the back seat, and someone appeared out of the shadows inside the gate. They talked a moment, then the guy from the inside unlocked and opened the chain link gate, and Pablo drove inside. They were locked back in.

"You can take off his blindfold now." Hunter rolled his eyes as the guy next to him did. For fuck's sake, he had his hands tied in front of him, he could have done it himself. LL needed a better crew.

Hunter looked around and saw they were at an auto body shop.

"The car doesn't look like it needs body work," Hunter noted.

He was met by silence. Seriously, these guys needed to buy a sense of humor. How did LL stand them? Just one more thing that went in the 'Con' column.

They all got out of the vehicle, Pablo untied him and motioned for Hunter to follow him. The guy who let him into the gate had it all—bald head, bandana, and neck tattoos—he couldn't be more 'gangy'.

"Howdy," Hunter said in English. This guy actually grinned.

"Hey, Tex," he replied in English. At last, a sense of humor, he could see why LL kept this one close. "You from Texas?" the man asked Hunter.

"Nah, just spent time with Texans. It rubs off," Hunter replied.

Gatekeeper switched to Spanish. "Let's hope you continue to keep LL amused, or you can deliver on your promise. I kind of like you. I'd hate to have to kill you."

"I'll keep that in mind," Hunter replied in Spanish.

Gatekeeper turned to Pablo, "I'll take him in to see LL. You wait here."

"But—"

The gatekeeper shut him down with a look. It was a good look, something Gray had perfected over the years. Hunter could do it with new recruits too.

"Follow me." Hunter followed him from the car bay doors into one of the grungiest garages he'd seen in a while. They bypassed the office doors on the left and went up the narrow staircase. At the top of the stairs, the gatekeeper knocked on the door.

"It's open."

He opened the door, and it was night and day. Except for the absence of a window, it looked like a high powered executive office. The desk was sleek glass and steel. There was a marble bar inset in wood-paneled walls. The floor was slate. There was a small conference table over to the side, and the seats all looked like leather. Hunter looked over at LL, who had an enthusiastic grin.

"Pretty swanky, right?"

"I'll say. You've moved up in the world."

"It pays to make a good impression. You wouldn't believe what kinds of fools I have to deal with. One look at this office and they immediately realize I know things they don't. They listen and fall into line."

It wasn't a bad idea on LL's part.

"What's your territory up to?"

"Took down The 15th Street Gang, The Machine, and took over *El Fuego*."

"What happened to Herman? I can't imagine you and he are co-managing the *Las Nuevas Espadas* unless of course, he got a lot prettier since I last saw him, and your tastes have changed."

The air in the room turned ominous. "You know, sometimes you're not as funny as you think you are, Man, you hearing me?" LL said.

"Got it. Now I know where the line is drawn. You still with Rita?" She and LL had a son before Hunter had left to join the Navy.

"Yeah," LL smiled. "You remember Lorenzo Junior? Well, we have five more kids now. God's blessed us."

"Lorenzo in the life?"

"Damn right. He's learning how to handle the girls. They love him."

If he was anything like his father, Hunter didn't doubt it, but it still made him sad. He couldn't be any more than seventeen. What kind of life was he living, handling a bunch of prostitutes?

"I see that look. You think you're all that because you're a SEAL?"

Hunter stilled.

"What, you didn't think I would keep track of my boy? You came in second in your BUD/S class. What was your problem? I expected first."

So had Hunter. Still pissed him off that Dalton had beat him.

"How d'you find out about that?"

"I told you, we've been busy. For a while, we did a little credit card fraud, so we had a hacker. I had him look you up."

Hunter didn't like the feel of that, he'd have to put Dex on the case.

"LL, I'm not judging how you're raising Lorenzo." Hunter paused. "Scratch that, maybe I am. Don't you want your son to have something better? Something outside of this life?"

"Look around you." LL waved his arm. "I've made something of myself. What more could the kid ask for? He's loving it. He'll have a great life."

"Or end up in prison or dead. You know you have a huge target on your back."

"Quit your preaching. That's not funny. You know I like it best when you're funny. Or when you have information. So be funny or give me information."

"How about this, you give me information, and I take down *Los Demonios* for you?"

LL looked at him, sizing him up. "Is this shit they say about SEALs for real?"

"We have our moments."

"Damn, you should have never left. You and I could have ruled this city."

"Again, you're not hearing me. I looked it over, the odds were I would be in prison or dead. Where is our old group, LL?"

The man got quiet and sat back in his chair.

"Come on," Hunter prompted. "There were seven of us. You ruled us. I was your second, we were little shits who reported up to Red Blade, but you led us. I got the fuck out, but what about the other five? What about Luther? Can you tell me what happened to him?"

"He's dead. He OD'd."

"What about Luis?"

"He's serving thirty over in Lancaster."

"The others?"

"Felix was shot, he's in a wheelchair. Alberto, he died in prison. But Bautista is still going strong, he's one of my lieutenants, just like you could have been," LL said it like it was something to celebrate.

"Great odds, LL. Great fucking odds." Hunter's words dripped with disgust. "Aren't you even sad about the others?"

"Aren't you? You left them? Maybe all that shit wouldn't have gone down if you'd been here to watch their back, you ever think about that?"

Fuck. Not this again.

"LL, it was their decision to stay. They could have left, same as me. As a matter of fact, I asked. No, I begged every fucking one of you to get the fuck out. To leave the life." He had. He'd begged LL the hardest. He'd been like a brother to him.

"Yeah, you were crazy."

"Sure I was, look at where they are today."

"Tell me, what are the odds of making it home as a SEAL? Last I heard, each and every one of you has a bounty on your head."

What the fuck? How did this guy know that kind of shit? It rarely made it to the public.

"I told you, I've been keeping tabs on you, Man."

"Why?"

"I wanted to see if what you said was true. I wanted to see if you really would make a life for yourself." LL eyed him, all humor gone. "Man, you only made half a life for yourself. Yeah, you're all that as a SEAL, but where's your woman? Where's your kids? Where's your family? You hardly even come home to see your grandmama."

"My team is my family."

"Do you fuck 'em?"

"Now who isn't being funny?" Hunter growled.

"Just saying. You need a wife. You need kids. You're missing out. That's why I checked on you, I cared."

God this trip was biting him in the ass.

"Well, if you've been keeping tabs on me, then you know that with a little help from some friends of mine, I can take care of your little rival gang."

"God, you always were a cocky bastard."

This time it was Hunter's turn to laugh. He kept laughing. LL joined in.

"Okay, we were both cocky," LL finally admitted. "Didn't you miss us a little?"

"Maybe to begin with, but I wanted to do the right things, LL. I wanted to be on the side of the angels. I wanted to serve my country. My teammates I served with are my brothers. The other teams we go on missions with, those men I would lay my life down for. The things we do, LL, they're important. We save lives."

"Tell that to Osama Bin Laden."

"And how many innocents are alive today because he's rotting at the bottom of the ocean?"

"Fine, you're a big bad SEAL. You're kind of still funny. I'm kind of believing you can help me with my *Los Demonios* problem, so I won't kill you."

"I need more than that."

"Want, want, want. Need, need, need. It's never-ending."

"I take it you have daughters?"

"Yep, you guessed it," LL laughed. "Five of them. Lorenzo is my only boy. So, what do you need?"

"I need all the information you have on a guy named Mateo and how he fits into *Los Demonios* hierarchy."

"I can get that information. I should have it tomorrow night, Friday at the latest."

"Sounds good."

"Do you need a ride somewhere? You grandmother's place?"

Hunter hated that LL knew where *Mamie* lived, but that was the problem when you had people who'd known you since grade school. "Yeah, I could use a lift."

"Martin!" LL yelled. The door immediately opened. The gatekeeper walked in, he must have been standing at the top of the stairs. "You drive my friend Hunter to where he wants to go. I don't want those other idiots knowing too much about my old friend."

"Got it, boss."

"Hunter, give me your number. I might have some information about you, but that I don't have."

Hunter rattled it off, and LL gave him his.

"I'll be calling," LL said.

"Appreciate it."

"If you come through, we'll be even. Even for your desertion fourteen years ago."

How was it that LL saw it as desertion, and Hunter saw it as the smartest move he'd ever made? The one in the wheelchair? The one in the state pen? The dead one? Or God forbid, LL's lieutenant. Nope, it was the smartest move in the world.

CHAPTER SIX

Oh God her head felt like it was inside a church bell on Sunday morning with Quasimodo ringing the damn thing. She did not have a concussion. She did not have a concussion. She did not have a concussion.

She raised her head off the pillow and realized it was probably for the best her grandmother had checked on her as often as she had throughout the night. Dammit, she didn't like this, but the doctor said this would be the worst day, and by Saturday, she should be feeling better.

Okay, now where was the aspirin? She got up gingerly from the bed and tiptoed down the hallway to the bathroom. Opening the medicine cabinet, she found some extra strength Tylenol. Thank the Lord. She didn't even bother going to the kitchen, she swallowed them dry.

She tiptoed past her grandmother's room on the way back to her own, laid back down, and considered yesterday's events. First had been the calls with the police detectives and the insurance adjusters. Then, she considered the call with her principal, Bill, they just discussed when she would return to work. She had plenty of sick time, and Bill wanted to wait for her bruising to clear up. When she protested, they agreed she could call in, and they would send over a new laptop since hers was destroyed in the bombing, so she could work online. That conversation was pretty mundane. But the conversation with Hunter? That was an earthquake.

She'd replayed those minutes in the kitchen over and over in her head all night long, which is probably the real reason for her headache, she hadn't gotten any sleep. During the night she'd made up her mind to talk to Hunter about Nicolas. She needed to protect her mother and grandmother and she knew in her heart that Hunter would figure out a way to help her help the young man as well.

But that wasn't the real reason she couldn't sleep. Now that she had decided to rely on Hunter, that meant that he would be in her life for the time it took to resolve things, and it scared her. She'd told him to leave, just like she had thirteen years ago, but he wouldn't listen. She knew the woman he would eventually find beneath the surface, and she was a hell of a lot more scarred than the one her dad had found to be such a unimaginable hardship. She really wanted Hunter to leave with good memories of her. The fact that he saw her as beautiful told her how flawed his thinking was. What was she going to do?

"*Láska*, do you want breakfast?"

"I'll be out in a moment, *Babička*." She got up and dressed. Thank God Lottie had finally come to her senses and brought over something loose for her to wear.

It wasn't until she was down the hall and face-to-face with Hunter that she realized her grandmother had been speaking in English.

"Hunter?" It was as if her thoughts had conjured him.

"I told you I was going to stay and watch over you and your grandmother. I'm going to look in after your mom later on today."

"But—"

He took a step toward her, and she held her ground.

"*Cariña*, I told you I wasn't leaving. Not this time."

"Why?" she burst out softly, so her grandmother wouldn't hear.

"I left part of me when I left you."

They stood there staring at one another. Aliana didn't know how to respond.

Her grandmother broke the silence. "I'm making waffles, with marionberry jam. I made the jam myself."

"That sounds wonderful, Mrs. J. What can I do to help?"

"You could take out the trash." Her grandmother pointed to the cupboard under the sink. Hunter bent to it and pulled out the trash bin.

"Is there anything else? Recycling?"

"Yes, that's near the washer and dryer. The trash cans are under the carport."

"Got it."

Aliana watched his economical movements that had his muscles bunching under his gray T-shirt. As soon as he was safely out of the kitchen, she turned to her grandmother.

"When did he get here?"

"I called him in when I was making coffee this morning."

"What do you mean, you called him in?"

"He spent the night in his car, watching our house."

"Actually, I didn't," Hunter said as he came back in the door. He smiled, and Aliana remembered his smile from years ago. So white in his dark face. His dimples showed. She'd always loved his dimples. She shook her head to clear it.

"So you weren't watching over us?" She felt let-down.

"I had to go search for Mateo, so I had one of my teammates watch your place. He's a SEAL too, so I trust him."

As soon as Mateo's name was mentioned, Aliana couldn't catch her breath. How in the world had Hunter found out about him?

"How do you know about…?" Her voice trailed off.

"You had some visitors yesterday evening. I think it was the *Los Demonios*' version of the welcome wagon. We had a friendly little talk, and they mentioned that Mateo was looking for you."

"They came here?" She took a shallow breath. "To my grandmother's house?"

He came and stood in front of her, gently placing his hands on her shoulders. Looking into his warm brown eyes calmed her.

"I'm sorry Alia, but yes, they came here. We talked about that possibility yesterday, remember?"

"I was hoping you were wrong, stupid of me, wasn't it?"

"Not stupid. Maybe naïve."

"Don't placate me. I screwed up, admit it. If I run around with my eyes closed while my home is blown up and my grandmother's house is being watched, I'm useless. I can't stand that. I need the truth."

His warm brown eyes darkened. "Well, so do I. Why the hell didn't you tell me that you'd been attacked?"

"Because I wasn't supposed to." *Sakra*, she didn't mean to admit to so much.

"You need to tell me, you and your family's lives are at stake."

She blew out a deep breath, "I'm going to, I promise. Just give me a minute to catch my breath." She gave him a pleading look.

"My God, you're stubborn. Well fine, it doesn't matter, I am planted firmly in the middle of your shitstorm, no matter what."

She looked up when her grandmother giggled.

"What?" she asked. "What's funny?"

"I learned a new idiom. Shitstorm. I like this one."

Aliana looked to heaven. God help her, everyone had gone crazy.

"*Babička*, I appreciate that you're going to learn great new terms from Hunter, but he needs to leave. Actually, we both do. We're going to check into a hotel." Why hadn't she thought of this yesterday?

"No. I'm not leaving my home. I want to stay." It was a bad sign when her grandmother put her hands on her hips.

"You don't understand—"

"I understand just fine," the older woman cut her off in Czech. "You're afraid of Hunter. Something has been broken in you since your father took his life. Hunter can fix it."

"What are you talking about? Hunter can't fix anything." She didn't address the part where she was broken or her father.

"No, that's not the truth, granddaughter. You've been living a half-life for too long. I'm not going to allow it anymore. You have to face your past and move on. This is a good, strong man who will keep you safe. You need him. Face your demons and walk into the light, beautiful girl."

Tears threatened to fall.

"Okay, enough of this happy horseshit. I don't know what's being said, but you crying isn't acceptable."

"I'm liking him, *Láska*," her grandmother switched to English. "Happy horseshit means you're unhappy, yes?" she asked, turning to Hunter.

"God save me," He muttered. "Look Aliana, I'm sorry I said you were naïve. I'm sorry I got mad that you didn't tell me you were attacked. I have a lot of stress right now. Would you like to hear about it?" Oh God, he was giving her a half smile. He was up to something. She remembered this from years ago.

"Say what you need to say." She crossed her arms.

"I have my grandmother's book club meeting on Saturday, and they want me there. Why? Because they will have checked their little old lady network to find out who might have set the bomb in your apartment. Then, I have your grandmother wanting me to educate her in all the 'less than appropriate' terms I've learned since being in the Navy. You gotta just let me help you. Come clean to me, I'm begging you."

His brown eyes sparkled. He used to do the same thing whenever she was close to tears or actually in tears back in school. He would do crazy things or make up wild stories to make her laugh. Anything so she would feel better.

"Your *Mamie* doesn't really have a book club, does she?" She hadn't just asked that, had she? She wasn't actually suckering in, was she?

"Swear to God." He held up three fingers like a boy scout would.

"And they're meeting on Saturday and invited you?"

"Yep."

She narrowed her eyes. He had to be kidding her. "If this is true, I want to come."

"Thank you." He reached down and cupped her cheeks. "Thank you, thank you, thank you. The way *Mamie* was talking up Velma's German chocolate cake, I was worried she was trying to fix us up."

Aliana sputtered out a laugh. The man was outrageous. Out came the dimples. She tugged his hands, pulling them away from her cheeks. He held them clasped in his hands. She was aware of every moment they touched. She thought about the letter he wrote her when he left. Those words had touched so much more than just her body, they'd touched her soul.

"Why are you frowning, have you changed your mind already, *mi Cielieto*?"

Aliana rolled her eyes. "Just because I'm trying to take the high road and deal with our situation today in order to make sure *Babička* is okay doesn't mean I'm going to fall for your bullshit every time you start peddling it, you got me?"

They both laughed at her, and she knew she was doomed.

Her grandmother turned to the counter and poured batter into the waffle iron.

"Should I get the bacon out of the fridge?" Hunter asked her.

"After you wash your hands," her grandmother replied.

Aliana watched as they cooked breakfast like a well-oiled machine. Her world was changing before her very eyes. Hunter just made himself at home, and she was allowing herself to like it. This had to stop. Twenty-four hours. It's only been twenty-four hours.

She got up and cleared off the table and set it. When she went to get the butter out of the fridge, Hunter was slipping by to get the cheese for the eggs. He gave her a lazy smile, making her tummy flip over. Must be the concussion, she assured herself.

They all sat down to breakfast, her grandmother sat across from her, which left her sitting next to Hunter. He watched what she put on her plate. Then added two pieces of bacon.

"I can't eat all of that."

"Yes, you can," he said.

"You're too slim," her grandmother chimed in.

"I am not. I'm in the weight range for my height."

"Bet you're on the low side," he said softly.

She ignored him. He was right, but she maintained her weight now. She no longer let it fall to an unhealthy level. She took a bite of her jam smothered waffle, flavor bursting in her mouth. "This is to die for. Thank you."

"I know your favorites, *Láska*."

"What does *Láska* mean?" Hunter asked.

"It means love," her grandmother answered. "I used to call my Terez that all the time, remember, Honey?" she asked Aliana. She nodded. Her grandfather had been bigger than life. She remembered him working at the forge in the foundry. All that molten metal fascinated her as a little girl.

When breakfast was over, Hunter said he needed to go back out to his car. "People need to see me, and I need to see what's going on. Before I go, Aliana, can you come out to the parlor with me? I want to ask you a couple of questions about Mateo."

She blanched. The cat was out of the bag. *Babička* would love that saying, she thought. But she would probably end up saying the dog was out of the bag. Since he knew who Mateo was, he was going to find the connection to Nicolas soon enough, wouldn't he? She bit her lip, then hissed. She needed to stop doing that, it was a bad habit even when she wasn't injured.

She got up and they went and sat down on the couch in the parlor.

"Ernie told me you needed stitches. Was it Mateo, who cut you?"

Ping. Ping. Ping. Her buttons hit the cement.

Strong hands cradled hers. Warmed them.

"Alia, stay with me. You're safe. Tell me what happened."

She shook her head. She'd tell him about Mateo, but she didn't want to relive her attack. Her braid whipped around and hit her face. He tugged it away and brushed it back over her shoulder.

"You can tell me anything. Don't you remember? You told me what those girls did to you in the bathroom. I took care of it. Remember?"

"I hated telling you. It was so hard," she whispered hoarsely.

"Ah, *mi Cielieto*, my heart was breaking. I looked all over for you. When I found you huddled up under the bleachers, there was no way I was letting you get away with not telling me."

She remembered that. He was looking at her the same way now, wanting to know about Mateo.

"Alia, please stop crying."

"Go away, Hunter." She grabbed her knees tighter, making sure her legs were covered by her skirt. It was the only practical thought she'd had since Lupita, Heather, and Theresa slammed open her bathroom stall.

"What happened? What's wrong?"

"Nothing. Go away."

"Is it those bitches? What did they do?"

He knew that they had been calling her a fat, ugly foreigner. He knew they passed notes and crude drawings of her around the classroom. Stuff like this had been going on all through elementary school, but Hunter had been able to intervene. Seventh and eighth grade, she'd had to go through it alone. Heather and Lupita were vicious, she had the bruises and the bad grades to prove it. But sometimes Hunter would be waiting to walk her home. Those were the best days.

Ninth grade things escalated and brought Theresa into the group. Hunter being a Junior was able to see it first hand, and he got involved almost every day. But he couldn't help now, there was no way she could ever tell anyone about this humiliation.

"You have to tell me."

She kept her face shoved against her folded arms. That was when he did something that hadn't happened since elementary school, he put his arm around her and started to rock her. It made her cry harder.

"Shhhh, it's going to be all right."

But it wasn't. It would never be all right again. She shuddered against him. She was so cold, and he was so warm. She shivered some more and tried to pull away. God, if he ever found out, he'd be disgusted just like the girls were. She needed to get her crying under control. She needed to get home somehow. She couldn't walk home. It was windy. She needed her father to come drive her home because he had their only car, but he didn't get off work until an hour after school got out. She'd just hide here until then.

"Please, go away."

"If I go away, I'm going to go find Lupita and Heather and demand to know what went down."

Her head jerked up. "No! You can't!" They'd show him. Then he wouldn't be her friend anymore. "Promise me you won't."

"Then, Alia, you have to tell me what happened." Sometimes he used his grown-up voice. Since she came to high school, she noticed he did it now and again. It must have happened when he got the tattoos. She liked them, and she didn't like them. She knew it meant he was involved with a gang. She didn't like that, but he was still her gentle Hunter. Her protector.

"Please don't make me," she said in a last-ditch effort to stop the inevitable.

"I'm just going to go ask the bitches." He sounded so different. So harsh.

Maybe if she spoke in Spanish, it wouldn't seem as real. It would be as if it happened to someone else. "

I went to the girl's restroom after the lunch period was done. I waited until it had cleared out. I always wait until everybody is pretty much gone."

"Why?" he asked in Spanish.

"I don't like being in there with the other girls." She didn't want to tell him why.

"Why?" he persisted.

"Because," she burst out," they always call me fat. They make fun of my clothes. All right?"

"Do they touch you?"

"They used to pull on my hair. That's why I wear it in a bun now."

He nodded like he wasn't surprised.

"So you went to the bathroom. Then what happened?"

"I heard Heather outside my stall telling someone to keep watch. I was still…you know… I tried to hurry. But then I thought I didn't want to go out there."

He looked at her, he was angry, but at the same time, he was soothing as he kept his arm around her shoulders. She appreciated the fact that he didn't prod her along, he waited for her to tell him at her own speed. She remembered the crash of the stall door banging open, the metal door hitting the inside wall. She was still sitting on the toilet. She squeezed her legs together, her panties around her ankles, she had her long skirt covering herself.

"I screamed at them to get out. It was Theresa and Heather who crowded in with me, Lupita was outside the stall, laughing."

Even when the dirt had suffocated her back in the first grade, she'd never been so scared. The two girls loomed over her. She stared up, grateful she had stopped peeing. She needed to wipe.

"Fatty's going to cry," Heather said in a singsong voice.

"Who cares. Look, it's just like you said. Look at those ugly undies." Heather bent down and yanked her panties over her shoes. She held them up by the tips of her fingers.

"Look, they have holes. I told you she would have the ugliest undies in school. Smelly too."

Aliana stared at them in horrified disbelief. This couldn't be happening. This couldn't be happening. Her panties didn't smell.

She was in charge of laundry at home. But it was true, they had holes in them.

"They're granny panties. Look at how big they are. They're ugly as fuck," *Heather crowed.*

"Wait 'til we show the others. We'll win for sure."

This couldn't be real. Say it wasn't happening.

"Thanks, Alley Fat, we've won the bet. We're going to win for finding the Ugly Undies for sure," *Lupita smirked.*

"Come on, let's show everybody our prize."

As soon as she heard them leave, she jumped up and tried to lock the door. The lock was broken. She did the best she could to clean up while holding the door shut. Trembling and shaking, she left the stall and went to wash her hands. She couldn't look at herself in the mirror.

She was halfway to the door when her stomach rebelled. She ran to another stall and bent over and everything she'd eaten for lunch came bubbling up and out. Again and again, she heaved. Snot came out her nose, her eyes watered. When she was done, she went to the sink and tried to clean up again, this time forced to look in the mirror. They were right, she was Alley Fat. She was pathetic. She needed a place to hide. Everybody was in class. She knew where to go.

"Jesus, I'll kill them."

"You would never hit a girl, Hunter."

"I'll make an exception." *She had never seen him so angry.* "Come on, I'm driving you home. Don't come to school for the rest of the week. It'll be taken care of by Monday."

Her eyes got wide. "But you don't hurt girls, not ever."

"I'm not. But those bitches are going down."

"Others will take their place. Mama and Papa won't let me dress like the other kids. I still talk funny. I try not to talk with an accent, but they only let me speak Czech at home. And I'm fat. It doesn't matter what you do."

"You're not fat. There's a lot of girls in this school who weigh as much as you do and people don't call them fat."

"That's because they're popular. They don't dress funny. I'm always going to be the funny dressing, funny talking, fat girl."

"Stop talking like that! You're special, Alia. You've always been special."

She felt like crying again. He was so wrong. But maybe if someone like Hunter thought she was special, then maybe she might be close to normal.

"So, do we have a deal?"

"Huh?"

"I drive you home. You call in sick. I take care of things."

She bit her lip. What choice did she have? If she told a teacher or the principal, it would just get worse. She nodded. Hunter squeezed her shoulder.

"You're brave Alia. You're special and brave."

"You need glasses."

* * *

"You were remembering, weren't you?"

She looked up and saw the grown-up Hunter. Somehow, she didn't remember it happening, she was crushed up beside him. He hadn't moved, but his arm was around her, and he was stroking her shoulder. She nodded her head.

"I can help you now like I did back then." His voice was rich and gentle.

"You have girl gang members you can sic on the bitches in my life?" She hiccoughed a wet laugh. "As I remember it, Rita was pretty darn vicious."

When she got back to school that following Monday, Lupita and Theresa showed up wearing scarves over their heads, and they refused to look at her. It wasn't until Tuesday that Heather arrived in a wig which somewhat imitated her blonde hair. That was when everyone caught on that all three of the girls were bald. It was confirmed when Jose Garmin tugged off Heather's bad blonde wig in first period and Lupita's scarf during lunch. The 'Alley Fat' days ended for a while, and instead 'Bald Bitches', 'Shaved Skanks' and 'Hairless Whores' were the butt of all the jokes.

Hunter laughed outright. "God Aliana, you were always braver than you knew. I love that you can laugh about that now."

"What are you talking about? I hid behind you."

"Laughter through tears, right? I've been there, got the T-shirt."

"You cry?" She couldn't picture it.

He got a faraway look in his eye. "I cried for you that day."

She stared at him stunned. Finally, she got her voice. "But not since you grew up, right?"

He frowned. Then ever so gently, he brushed a stray tear from her cheek. "What kind of man would that make me if I hadn't felt strongly enough about things to cry about them?"

He was remembering something really bad. She could see the sorrow in his eyes. She hated it. She reached out and for the first time, *she* touched *him*. Cupping the side of his face, she gave him a soft smile.

"Thank you for being there for me. You made a difference in my life. I couldn't have survived without you, Hunter."

"You got it wrong, I couldn't have survived without you."

He made her feel like a heroine from a novel. How was that possible?

He cleared his throat. "You have to tell me about Mateo. I need to know what happened."

She bowed her head. He was right.

"I guess it's no different, you know almost all the ugly parts of my life."

"*Chaquita*, one day you'll learn you can tell me *all* the ugly, and it won't matter."

How she wished that were true.

"Mateo and three of his friends jumped me in the parking lot outside of my townhome. The security cameras had been vandalized two days before. I couldn't help but wonder that it might have been planned." She was proud how even her voice sounded. Now if she could just keep it that way.

"Four men?"

"Not men, exactly, more like boys. Students."

"Really? Mateo is twenty-one, isn't he? That qualifies as a man in my book," Hunter said harshly.

"Anyway, before I could get to the pepper spray in my purse, one of them came up behind me and jerked both up my arms up behind my back. I was worried he was going to dislocate my shoulders."

Still calm. She could do this.

"Fucker."

"Mateo pulled out a knife. He put it against my throat. I knew he wasn't going to kill me." Damn, she heard her voice shake just a little. "He made a lot of noise about how I needed to stop encouraging Nicolas."

"Let me guess, you argued." Hunter's eyes glittered down at her.

She didn't respond, she knew better. "For some reason, Mateo escalated."

"Goddamn it, Alia, you're the reason he escalated. You should have just agreed with him." Hunter reached out and touched the small bandage on her throat. "Then what happened. How did he escalate?"

"He… He…"

Hunter tugged her close, then tipped up her chin. "Tell me *Cariña.*"

"He told me exactly where my mom lived. He threatened to kill her. He knew the facility and even what room she was in. Then he cut off my shirt and bra. The end." There, she got it out without breaking down. Her lips tilted up in a semblance of a smile.

"Try that again, Alia." Hunter looked exactly like he had under the bleachers. She could feel the rage pouring off him.

"The details don't matter."

"They matter. Tell me."

She rubbed her chest and winced. He pulled her hand away and pulled her into his arms, just like she'd asked him to at the start.

"Please tell me, *mi Cielieto*," he coaxed. "You have no idea what I'm imagining."

"I was scared," she said quietly. "I didn't want to be. I wanted to be strong."

He stroked her hair, and she pressed tighter against him.

"One of them, he said…he said I had 'nice tits', I prayed I wouldn't be raped."

"Motherfucker," he whispered fiercely into her hair. Somehow that made her feel better, and she continued.

"Mateo kept saying I had to stop giving Nicolas motivation. He said that his family was the gang."

Hunter laid his cheek on her head. "And you disagreed."

"I had to, Hunter."

"Of course you did. Then what happened?"

"He threatened to kill my mother. I told you he knew where she lived, even knew there was a tree right outside her window. And then…"

"Then what?"

"That's when he used the tip of his knife to cut the buttons off my blouse."

"How did he end up cutting your chest, *mi Cariña?*"

"He slipped the knife under my bra, I don't think he meant to cut my chest, but one of the other boys—"

"Men," Hunter interrupted. "They were men, Alia."

"One of the others said they heard a siren, and Mateo ended up cutting the bra and my chest. Then they shoved me into my car, and they all ran away."

"Mother, mother, fuckers."

She didn't tell him about the medal. She just couldn't. That was private. She swallowed.

"*Cariña*, I have to go. I have a friend who's due to arrive soon. He's going to spell me, and now that I know about this, I'll go check in on your mom."

"Can I go with you?"

"You've been rubbing the back of your neck and your temple for the last half hour. Why don't you take a nap and see how you feel afterward? If you feel up to a drive to Glendale after that, then sure."

He searched her eyes and must have seen something that assured him because he leaned over and kissed her forehead. He smelled good. She wrapped her arms around him. He felt good.

"I'll call you."

"You don't have my number."

"Yes, I do," he winked at her, then left.

CHAPTER SEVEN

Dalton and Zed were outside, Starbucks coffee cups in their hands, standing next to his bike. They both had knowing smirks on their faces. What the fuck? They'd never met before and they looked like they were in cahoots.

"I didn't know you'd be here so early from Virginia," he said to Zed. "How'd you know where to come?"

"I texted Dalton when I landed. I figured you'd be busy." He motioned to the other man who was leaning over his bike and touching the chrome. He always did that, knowing that Hunter didn't like people touching his motorcycle.

"He was right. You sure were in the house a long time. How long does it take to tell Aliana and Mrs. Jankovic that you were going to visit Mrs. Novak?" Dalton gave him a sly smile.

Hunter scowled, and both men laughed. "Seriously, you both need to get lives. As for Aliana, I just want to finally get some closure." Their laughter continued.

"Believe what you need to believe. Hell, I haven't even seen her, and I know better than that, she has you tied up in knots," Dalton said.

"You Black Dawn guys are slow," Zed asked Dalton. "I had the good sense to pull her up online, I got a look at her. I can see what has our boy worked up. Add in their past history…?" Zed let his voice trail off.

Hunter raked his hand through his hair. "Shut it. Here comes Mrs. Price. I really don't need this shit from you two in front of her." He turned and smiled at the woman as she crossed the quiet residential street.

"Hello, Hunter, I was hoping these two men were your friends. I brought prune Danish. It's good for your digestion." She had a department store shopping bag that she handed to Hunter. He held it open for her. She took out paper plates and handed them to Dalton. She handed the forks to Zed, then handed him an oversized Tupperware container. Then she looked coyly at Hunter.

"I have two thermoses in here. One with the coffee I know you like, and another with milk. My husband likes milk with his Danish. There are plastic cups inside too."

"You're doing too much Mrs. Price," Hunter protested. "Mrs. Jankovic just made me breakfast."

"What did she fix?"

"Waffles."

"With her homemade jam?"

"Yes."

"Well, this is my homemade prune Danish recipe, you'll have to tell me which you like better."

"If I answer that question, Mrs. Price, then I won't keep getting food from both of you, and I'm not a stupid man."

"You're right, you are a smart man." She had a nice laugh. "That's something my Bernie would say. Return the thermoses and Tupperware when you're done, and I'll fill them back up later." She gave a wave and left.

"This is the cushiest assignment I've ever been on," Dalton said.

"You got waffles?" Zed asked. "With homemade jam?"

Hunter grinned and nodded.

"How do we get in on that? Not that I don't appreciate prunes," Dalton said. He was pouring coffee into his empty Starbuck's cup. Hunter waited to see his expression as he took a sip.

"Shit! You could have warned me. Give me that milk."

Hunter laughed. "Serves you right for gossiping like a little old lady."

"Well, that's now officially over with. What's on the agenda for today?"

"A guy named Mateo, who hangs with the *Los Demonios* gang, has attacked Aliana. He cut her. It required stitches. It happened a week ago. She hasn't told the cops everything."

"Dammit. We need to take that fucker down. Why isn't she talking cops?" Zed demanded. "Go back in there and tell her she needs to cooperate with the police."

"Hey, throttle back." Hunter remembered what Zed had said about his last assignment. "He threatened her mom. I'm going over and checking her status at the nursing home she's in over in Glendale. I'll do that a little later today. Alia wants to go with me, but we'll see how she's feeling after her nap."

"So what else is on tap?" Dalton asked, trying to smooth things out.

"Checking in with her friend, Lottie, and see if there is anything to the fact that she has expelled four gangbangers this semester. That's the excuse she's given the police for the bomb. This Mateo is the guy who came after her, but how else could she have caught his eye, but at the school?"

"Makes sense. So, what time are we questioning Lottie?" Zed asked. Damn, Zed was all in.

"I haven't called her yet."

"Get to it," Zed commanded him. If his friend didn't mellow, he was going to have to get him drunk, laid, or just beat the shit out of him.

"Who says you're going to be going with Hunter?" Dalton asked.

"I've just spent far too long in a cramped plane. I'm pulling rank, Sullivan. You're babysitting, while I go out with Diaz."

"Okay, maybe I can talk Mrs. Jankovic into giving me some waffles," Dalton smiled.

Hunter glowered at Dalton.

"Hey, I'd eat them here on the street, so I could watch what was going on. I could sit on your bike," Dalton said.

"I'm going to take your 'vette out for a spin as soon as we get home, and I'm going to eat powdered sugared jelly donuts in it while I'm driving," Hunter replied.

"Hey, no need to get violent," Dalton said, holding up his hands.

"Quit it you two. Hunter, call Lottie. We need to get a move on."

"I guess this isn't your op anymore," Dalton grinned.

"He's an old man, he can't help but think he's in charge," Hunter concurred.

"I'm not so old I can't take the two of you," Zed growled.

Hunter looked at his friend and mentor and realized that despite his earlier laughter, he was wound tight. This did not bode well for Ms. Carlotta Rodriguez. He saw Dalton's eyes make a quick move, and he gave a slight chin tilt. As always, they were on the same wavelength. Hunter pulled out his phone and called the number he had gotten from Mrs. J.

"Ms. Rodriguez, this is Hunter Diaz."

"Hi. I see you're punctual," she said brightly.

"I beg your pardon?"

"I thought you would want to question me about our friend. It would be best if we didn't do it here at the school. Ever since the explosion, I can't stop eating. I want good food, and I know just the place. There's a taco truck on La Meda and Conway. Can we meet there?"

"We'll be there in a half hour."

"Make it twenty." She hung up. He grinned. Now they had a reason not to take Zed's rental car.

"We have a meet, it's a taco truck on La Meda and Conway, she wants us there in twenty."

"It's thirty minutes, maybe more depending on traffic."

"Not with the right rides. Where's your sense of adventure?" Hunter asked.

Zed gave him a considering look. "What do you have in mind?"

"Since you're older, I'll give you a leg up. I'll give you the bike. I'll take Dalton's piece of shit truck. The last one there buys."

Zed's eyes glittered at the challenge. He held out his hand for the keys, at the same time dumping the items Mrs. Price had given him back into the shopping bag. Hunter handed over his keys and gave Dalton the shopping bag. Zed got into the saddle and fired the motorcycle to life.

"She sounds good, Hunter," he grinned. He put on the helmet and pulled away from the curb.

"Well, that should put the Chief in a better mood. You gonna let him win?" Dalton asked.

"Fuck no. Give me your keys."

Dalton tossed them over, and Hunter took off at a run toward Dalton's truck. Hell, he knew the streets better than Zed, he'd been here more recently, and this truck rocked.

* * *

Hunter would have won if he could have found a parking spot. When he got there, Zed was talking to Lottie, and it was clear he was admiring her. She was all that in her pinstripe suit and red heels. Hell, the boys must be lining up to get 'counseling'. He took in the fact her plate was loaded. He bet she got a hell of a lot more than the normal serving and slow service, so they could keep her longer at the window.

"There he is. I see you lost," she said. "I'm trying to talk your friend Zed into getting something to eat."

Hunter noticed Zed seemed more relaxed, he couldn't tell if it was Lottie or the bike ride.

"Aren't you hungry?" Hunter asked.

"After we ask our questions. Ms. Rodriguez is on a tight schedule, right?"

She'd taken a bite of food as they meandered to one of the nearby benches, so she just nodded. She and Zed sat down. Hunter leaned against the armrest on the other side of her.

"We need to ask you a few questions," Hunter said.

"Ask away," she waved her fork and smiled.

"Alia said she expelled some gang members who might be holding a grudge. Do you think they would want to bomb her house?"

"All four of them showed up with guns. One Brainiac had his tucked in his waistband and shot himself in his ass. He was in study hall with his friends when it happened, and they tried to scatter. The homeroom teacher is the football coach, he stopped them."

"All three of them?"

"Oh yeah, he got them all. He used to play pro ball for the Los Angeles Rams," she grinned. "By the way, call me Lottie. We're all on the same team."

"So, teammate, who do you think had a hand in blowing up Aliana's townhome?" Hunter asked baldly.

"Ernie asked me the same thing."

"Who's Ernie?" Zed asked.

"He's the cop who found Aliana after she was attacked last week."

"Kid, you've left a few things out of your report. I need to know all the players," Zed said to Hunter.

Hunter managed to stop himself from rolling his eyes. Seriously, Zed needed to learn how to step into the buddy zone and stop trying to run things. Goddammit, he wasn't on the Night Storm team, he was a member of Black Dawn. Aiden was his second-in-command, not Zed.

"What did you tell Ernie?" Hunter asked.

"He asked me about a boy named Mateo. He used to go to school here, dropped out his senior year. Aliana was a teacher back then, and she taught him when he was a sophomore. She told me about him."

"Were you close back then?" Zed asked.

"No, I wasn't working at the school back then. I showed up three years later." Lottie took another delicate bite of her enchilada.

Hunter waited for her to finish swallowing to ask her his next question.

"If you weren't working here, what made him stand out so much she would be telling you about him years later."

"His younger sister used to attend school here, and her brother is currently a student. His sister Darla is a pet project of mine, and Nicolas is a pet project of Aliana's."

"Explain," Zed commanded.

"I'm not under your command," Lottie said gently.

"Look, we're under a time crunch," Zed said irritably.

"Good manners don't take extra time," Lottie said as she took a bite of rice.

Shit, the bike ride hadn't mellowed Zed out.

"Lady, I'm just—"

"We're just trying to help Aliana, and we're on edge," Hunter said, trying to smooth things over.

"No, you're doing fine Hunter." Lottie wiped her mouth. "Zed isn't." She gave Zed a thoughtful look. "What happened? If I had to guess, you just had to deal with some bad ju-ju."

"Ju-ju?" Zed's eyebrow shot up.

"I use the term with the kids a lot. It's another word for shit. You just went through some bad shit, and the rest of us are paying for it. Have you talked to someone about it?"

"Are you a shrink?" He eyed her, consideringly.

"Yep. Got the piece of paper to prove it."

"Fuck me. You talk to her Hunter." Zed stole a chip off of Lottie's plate, and she laughed.

"You were telling us about Mateo's siblings?" Hunter prompted.

"We know Mateo is in *Los Demonios*. He recruited his younger brother Nicolas, but Nicolas is really gifted. His teachers brought him to Aliana's attention. Chances are he can get a scholarship out of here if he continues on the path he's on now."

"That's great," Hunter smiled.

"But Mateo really wants him in the life. He puts a lot of pressure on him." She scowled. "Mateo is a cancer in that family."

"What makes you think that, is it because of Darla?"

"Two years ago, she got arrested and sent to juvie for attempting to stab a boy here at Bertrum. She's a troubled girl. I can't go into the whys and wherefores, but I'm not surprised Mateo's name came up."

"Can we talk to them?"

"Nicolas will be leaving school at three o'clock. I don't know if Darla is still living with her mother and Nicolas. I hope she is, she needs as much help as she can get. She's four months pregnant."

"How old is she?"

"Seventeen."

Both men winced.

"Have you made time to talk to Ernie?" Lottie asked.

"I'm surprised I didn't get a ticket from him on the way over here. Last time we talked, he said he would be watching me," Hunter said.

"Yeah," Lottie laughed, "it sounded like y'all had a regular old dick swinging match." Her grin was infectious. Hunter saw Zed's lip curl upwards. "You should. He's saying the bomb was real amateur hour."

"Well, thank God, that saved Aliana's life." Hunter couldn't imagine a world without Aliana Novak in it.

"No, you're not hearing me. It was done so poorly, he says it was almost purposeful that she didn't wind up dead. He thinks someone arranged it so that she lived."

Zed sat up on the bench. "Now that's interesting."

"I'd say you and Ernie should kiss and make up," Lottie said sweetly.

"He was on the list of people to call today," Hunter smiled easily. He was, but Lottie and Aliana's mother were higher up on the list.

"So, how come you know all of this, Carlotta?" Zed asked as he snagged another tortilla chip. This time he took some guacamole dip too.

"He and I have gone out a few times. He likes women with degrees on the wall," she gave him a sideways smile.

"Oh, there's a lot to like. I just don't need anyone crawling around in my brain," Zed said.

"Honey, if you don't think any woman you date isn't digging around in your deep dark places, you are out of your ever-loving mind." Zed's chip paused midway to his mouth. "Oops, I guess I hit too close to home."

"Keep it up, keep it up, *Chaquita*," he warned as he bit into the guac covered chip.

"I'm far from little," she frowned.

"It depends who you're comparing yourself to. Compared to me, you're tiny," Zed smiled easily. He turned to Hunter. "Do we have time to make it to Aliana's mother's facility before Nicolas gets out of school?"

"Yep."

"I'll give Ernie a call so he can be around to ticket you, it'll make his day," Lottie grinned.

Hunter reached over and helped himself to two chips and an even bigger helping of guacamole dip than Zed had taken.

"I'm going to be in town for a few days, seems to me I owe you a meal," Zed said as he got up off the bench.

"I don't play that way. I'm dating Ernie right now. But thanks for the offer. Totally made my day." She gave them both a salute.

Aliana got an A+ in friends.

* * *

Hunter and Zed walked away, and Hunter called Mrs. Jankovic's house to see if Aliana was awake yet. Aliana answered the phone and sounded much better.

"I definitely want to go to visit Mom. We're in luck because this is Shorinda's shift. She's in the know."

Hunter didn't quite understand what that meant, but figured he'd be in the know soon enough. Despite Lottie's threat, they still made stellar time getting back to Aliana. Zed won again, and Hunter rationalized it was because he was riding Hunter's Indian Chief Springfield motorcycle.

Aliana was waiting outside with Dalton and waved happily when she saw Hunter. It gave his heart a curious jolt. She walked over to him.

"You wear your hair down all the time now. You never used to do that," he said softly.

"I don't now, either. But wearing it up right now gives me a headache. I think it's a side-effect of the concussion."

"What if I told you I like it down?"

She bit her lip and winced. Then she licked it, and he winced.

"I suppose for the time you're here, I could wear it down. Except when I'm at school, of course."

"Of course," he agreed solemnly.

"We can take my car," she suggested. She pointed to the little hybrid under her grandmother's carport.

"I don't think so. Zed's cranky enough without asking him to fold into that. We'll take his rental."

"Oh, okay," she smiled. It was then he realized she thought they were going to be riding in Dalton's truck. He chuckled.

"You ever ridden on a motorcycle?"

"Of course not."

"After you're feeling better, we're going to have to change that."

"Quit your gabbing. We have to get this show on the road," Zed said.

"You're driving," Hunter said.

CHAPTER EIGHT

"Shorinda, this is Hunter and Zed," Aliana said.

The nurse's eyes were wide as she stared at the two men who towered over her. She swung her glance back at Aliana.

"Girlfriend, where have you been finding these men? Can I get a subscription? I have a little saved up. I've been a good girl." Then she turned back to look at the two men. "But I know how to be naughty," she teased with a slow smile.

Aliana knew she was turning forty-seven shades of red, but when she looked up at Hunter, his eyes were sparkling.

"Shorinda, I'm sure you are quite the package, but I'm loyal to my current subscriber." Holy hell, now she was going to need a fire extinguisher to put out her blush. They all saw it too, and even Zed was grinning at her. *Sakra.*

"Actually, they're here to help with the difficulty *Maminka* and I have been experiencing."

Shorinda's eyes went hard. "Don't think I didn't notice all these new bruises, little girl. What the hell happened? First, you come in with blood dripping off of you, and now you look like you've gone three rounds with Conor McGregor. Boys, you're not doing your job."

"We got into town after the bomb," Zed said.

"Bomb?" Shorinda screeched.

"Shhhhh, keep it down." Aliana looked over her shoulder to see her mother, her eyes wide open, looking at nothing. Still, just in case something might get through, she didn't want her to overhear the conversation.

"Bomb? Bomb? What the 'eff? Tell me what's going on. And you two, tell me how you're going to keep my girl and her Mama safe."

"We've got a 24/7 watch on Aliana, and we're here to see what kind of security this facility has."

"Basically, nothing. Did Aliana tell you about the threats to her mother?"

"Yes. She's made her confession."

"Shorinda, that's old news, okay?" Aliana gave her friend a hard stare. She looked around the new room and saw it was larger. "Does *Maminka* like the new room? Does it bother her being on the third floor?"

"Honey, she was happy two days ago."

"Shorinda, if money were no object, where would you put her mom for two weeks while this shit died down?" Zed asked, changing the subject.

"It's only going to take two weeks for you to get this settled?" the nurse asked.

"If that," Hunter said.

"Well then, I'd take two weeks vacation, rent a hospital bed, and bring her to my house. It's a three bedroom bungalow about fifteen miles from here. It's in a great little neighborhood, and I keep it neat as a pin. You're welcome to come see it before having your Mama come stay with me. And it's not a matter of money. I would charge the same amount as this place."

Then she paused and sighed. "But that's a pipe dream because there is no way I would make Aliana pay twice' she'd have to pay for her Mama's spot here, then pay me. That's not fair."

"Done," Zed said.

"What the hell are you talking about?" Hunter demanded. "I've got this covered."

"Boys," Aliana said, straightening up. "I appreciate what you're doing. I really do. But now that I know this is a two-week deal, of course, I have this covered." She looked over at Shorinda who shook her head.

"What?" Hunter demanded.

"There's taking charge, then there's being a steamroller." Aliana reached up and pushed back her hair so she could see both of the offenders clearly. "I think you and Tarzan haven't just crossed a line, I think you ran the race and managed to hit the finish line in the chauvinism race."

"It's sad, really," Shorinda said. "I keep forgetting all those beautiful muscles come with a price tag."

"How come I feel like I just met Vice Principal Novak?" Hunter asked.

"Welcome to my world Hunter," Aliana drawled. "I feel like I just met a Jarhead."

"Hey! Tarzan is acceptable, Jarhead is unacceptable. That's a Marine. We're Frogs," Zed said.

"That's not manly," Aliana frowned.

"Just roll with it girlfriend," Shorinda advised as she patted her arm. "I can take vacation starting tomorrow. I have so much saved up, they've been trying to boot my butt for months. This is perfect. I can get the ball rolling to coordinate the hospital bed and everything, and we can have her moved in twenty-four to forty-eight hours. You can arrange to have her signed out for a couple of weeks when you leave this afternoon. Now, go spend some time with your Mama while I entertain your admirers."

"They aren't my admirers," she protested.

"Your protectors then or the hot men who are standing here in front of me. I don't care what the hell we call them, let me talk to them while you talk to your Mama."

"Shorinda, I think it would be best if you don't objectify them. You should refer to them as Zed and Hunter." Aliana was using her professional training.

"Nope, I like being objectified. It makes the day go faster," Hunter laughed.

"I don't think Zed appreciates it," Aliana said primly.

"I bet you're hell on wheels as a Vice Principal. I sure as hell wouldn't have predicted this when I saw you sixteen years ago," Zed's voice was full of admiration.

"You saw me back then?"

He nodded. That made no sense. She thought back to who she was at twelve and cringed. Hunter must have seen it.

"Let's go say hi to your Mom," he said.

She looked over her shoulder at her Mother who currently looked catatonic. Introduce him? What was he talking about? But then again, she always believed part of what she said was getting through, even on nights like these.

"Okay."

He snuck his arm around her waist.

"*Maminka*, this is Hunter Diaz, do you remember him?"

She didn't move a muscle, not even batting an eyelash.

"She's not always like this. Sometimes she's asleep, sometimes she's awake. Sometimes she recognizes me." She wanted Hunter to understand her mother was so much more than who he was seeing at the moment.

"I know, *Cariña*." She saw they had an IV set up. That meant that her mother had either been like this for a while or while she was cognizant, she hadn't been eating. "Do you speak to her in English or Czech?" he asked.

"Czech."

"She sings to her," Shorinda called from across the room. Then she opened up a cupboard and brought Aliana her guitar. She looked at Hunter. "She sings like an angel."

Just how often could one person blush before their face became permanently red?

Hunter frowned. "I didn't know you played the guitar."

"*Babička* taught *Maminka* how to play, then she taught me. I guess it's a family tradition."

"Play one of the songs you wrote," Shorinda encouraged.

Aliana glared at her friend.

"I'm going to play one of *Maminka's* favorite songs, it's one she danced to at her wedding."

Aliana plucked at the guitar chords and soon lost herself in the music. She really liked this song, it talked about how the couple was meant to be together in both this life and the one after. She knew how much her mother loved her father, and for her sake, she hoped they would one day meet again, and it would be like it used to be when Aliana was little and her dad was nice and kind. When she finished the last note, she looked down at her mother and saw a single tear dripping down her temple.

"Hunter, do you see?" She grabbed his forearm excitedly. "I think she heard me."

"I see, *mi Cielieto*." She warmed at the endearment. He reached up and touched her flushed cheek. "I love this blush. I know when you have strong feelings. You are a slice of heaven. You know that, don't you?"

She ducked her head. He tilted up her chin.

"Sing another song," he requested. "You have a beautiful voice."

Sakra, her blush got hotter. She'd gotten many compliments in college, but none meant more to her than Hunter's praise. How could he have come to mean so much to her again?

Because he was Hunter Diaz, her heart whispered. He would always mean the world to her.

"We've got to go if we want to make it back to the school in time," Zed said.

She looked over at the other man, she had forgotten he was there. Shorinda was gone. She must have had to get back to other patients.

"School?" Aliana asked.

Zed walked over to them. "We're going to question Nicolas, and hopefully, he can take us to his sister. Better yet, that scum of a brother."

Aliana stood straighter. "Nicolas Garcia? My Nicolas? Why in the world would you be questioning him?" she demanded softly. She motioned for the two men to follow her toward the cupboard, so she could put away her guitar and not disturb her mother. She didn't want to have a knock-down-drag-out in front of her mom.

"Why didn't you tell us that Mateo was related to one of your students?" Hunter asked.

"I meant to, I just hadn't gotten to it." *Sakra*, how could she have forgotten? "How did you find out?" Then she sighed. "You talked to Lottie, didn't you?"

"Damn right we did, and it was nice that she was more forthcoming." Zed said menacingly.

"Back off," Hunter growled at Zed.

"Quit being so damn soft on her. She's a big girl. She's proved it."

"He's right, I am. I screwed up not telling you. But really he's not involved in this, not the way you're making this sound, Zed.". I don't want you questioning him. Full stop, end of story."

"Lady, you can't know that. He's probably part of this gang, so he knows."

"You're right, he is. But he's a good kid. He wants out."

"And you're just buying that? You're naïve." Hunter and Zed kind of looked alike, with their Mexican heritage, same dark hair, and brown eyes, but Zed's were looking almost black and cold, while Hunter's were a warm chocolate. Zed was pissing her off and she glared at him.

"Nicolas is only fifteen. He's not going to be questioned without a parent."

Zed snorted. "Let me guess, he's from a one parent home, and his mother is either working two jobs trying to keep things together, or she's strung out on drugs. Which is it?"

How the hell did he know that? "Two and a half jobs," Aliana admitted slowly. "Nicolas is incredible. His paper was a finalist in the Library of Congress literacy contest. That and the scores I expect him to have on his SATs, he'll be recruited by colleges."

"Only if a Vice Principal I know happens to be making a lot of phone calls on his behalf," Hunter teased gently. At least this time, she didn't blush because dammit, of course, she was going to make those calls. Nicolas deserved it.

"Anyway, he wouldn't know anything about my townhome being bombed."

"He has information about his brother, and don't tell me he doesn't know anything about *Los Demonios*," Zed said.

"He's a straight-A student," she hedged.

Zed laughed. "Did I tell you I grew up not fifteen minutes from Bertrum High School? I belonged to a gang. I joined when I was twelve. I got As and Bs. I don't even want to get into what I was doing by the time I was fifteen." He sounded sad and bitter.

"I'm so sorry, Zed."

"I'm not looking for sympathy. I'm trying to explain about gang members. Don't stereotype us."

She looked over at Hunter. She'd known him when he was seventeen in a gang. He hadn't been that way.

"Zed's right," Hunter said to her.

"We need to talk to Nicolas, Aliana, he knows things. There's no way he doesn't have knowledge if not some sort of involvement," Zed said. "We also need to talk to his sister."

She hoped these two men who got out of the life, could do a better job of helping Nicolas out than she had.

"Have you guys read Animal Farm?"

"Huh?" Zed said.

"I think so," Hunter said.

"He finalled in the Literacy Contest with a paper about Animal Farm. The book is about a pig named Napoleon, who is basically Stalin, and the other pig is Snowball, who is a compilation of Trotsky and Lenin. Nicolas compared the current gang leader of *Los Demonios* to Napoleon and he said he hoped he could be like Snowball and help overthrow the dictator-like leadership. He read this book six months ago. I think he's been doing things to disrupt the gang for awhile now. He just told me about it."

"Fuck me," Zed said.

"We've got to talk to him, quick," Hunter said.

"I know, I've tried to talk him out of it, but he's committed to the idea."

"We need to get to the school right now." Hunter put his arm around her waist. He did it gently, cognizant of her bruises. He looked down at her. "Say goodbye to your *Maminka*." Her heart melted that he used the Czech term for Mama. They walked over to her bed together. She bent over and brushed a kiss on her mother's warm, dry cheek.

"I love you, Mama. I'll see you soon," she said in Czech.

Hunter led her to the door where Zed was waiting. "We've got to hurry."

Their unease was blowing her anxiety levels through the roof. She felt like an idiot that she hadn't realized how explosive this situation was. Lottie wouldn't have made this kind of mistake.

Zed led the way, and Hunter took a moment to whisper in her ear.

"Don't beat yourself up."

"Lottie says I judge too much on stereotypes. She says I need to look deeper. I hate this."

"We all have our blind spots."

"I'm an educator. If I'm this naïve, maybe I should step down."

He halted them in the hallway. Zed stopped out of earshot, pointing to his watch. Hunter waved him away. "Are you always this hard on yourself?"

"I suppose."

"Is that a yes or a no?"

"It's a yes. But Hunter, these kids are important. They're in my care. Some of them have nobody in their corner. I have to stand up for them. If I'm this blind, then what use am I to them?"

"Are you or are you not helping Nicolas with his academics and a possible way out of East L.A.?"

"Yes, I'm helping him, but what will it matter if he ends up dead?"

"Did you learn from this? Will you have a better understanding of the next Nicolas?"

She slowly nodded.

"Well, there you go then. *Cariña,* you're too hard on yourself. It's a damn good thing I'm here to make sure you don't beat yourself bloody."

Aliana huffed out a breath. His words evoked different ways to get bloody, different ways to relieve the pressure, so she didn't feel like such a failure.

Be strong. You're past that.

"Alia, are you with me?"

"Huh?"

"You seemed in a daze."

"Just thinking of Nicolas. We better get going." They turned to Zed.

"About goddamn time. I'm going to have to do some creative driving in that piece of shit rental to make it. Now, get a move on."

* * *

Hunter watched as Aliana put her hair up in an intricate bun. She did it easily, without a mirror and with a few bobby pins she had in her purse. When she was done, it was as if she took on a whole new persona. She was now Ms. Novak. He didn't know if he was scared or put-off, but one thing was sure, he was sure as hell turned on.

For God's sake, the reason he had come back was he could no longer stand not knowing why she'd sent him away. She had been his best friend, in some ways, she had been his savior. Now here he was feeling lust? What the fuck? Get it together, Diaz.

They parked two blocks from the school. They all agreed having Zed or Hunter approach Nicolas would freak the kid out. They also thought because of Aliana's injuries, she couldn't approach Nicolas either, so she arranged to have Lottie bring him to them.

Nicolas was taller than Lottie by an inch even though she was wearing those ridiculous red heels. He was a good-looking kid. Didn't have that cocky attitude Hunter had been expecting, instead, he looked curious until he saw Aliana, then his entire demeanor changed.

"Ms. Novak, what happened? Are you all right? *Dios Mio*, should you be in a hospital? Sit down."

Right then, he knew he liked the kid. Aliana was standing outside the passenger door, and he opened it for her when he took note of Hunter and Zed. Nicolas ignored them for the moment and gave Aliana his hand to help her into the car.

"Nicolas, seriously, I'm fine," she laughed.

He crouched down in front of her. "Tell me what happened," he demanded.

She sighed and looked at Hunter in the backseat. "I see you were right, still waters run deep." She looked back at Nicolas. "My home was bombed three days ago."

"*Joder!*" Nicolas said with feeling.

"Nicolas," Aliana reprimanded.

"Leave the kid alone. Fuck is the appropriate word," Zed said.

"Who are these men?"

"They've come to protect me, my mom, and my grandmother."

Nicolas eyed her knowingly, sadly. "All of you have been threatened. By who?"

She didn't want to tell him. She couldn't.

"If you don't, I will," Hunter rumbled from the backseat.

She stayed silent.

"It was your brother, Mateo," Zed answered.

Nicolas closed his eyes and stood up. He walked away from the car. Hunter bolted out of the backseat.

Nicolas turned to face him. He looked him dead in the eye.

"I'm not leaving, I just need to think a minute," he said fiercely.

"Wanna take a walk?" Hunter asked in Spanish.

Nicolas nodded.

Hunter saw Lottie walk toward the car as he and Nicolas began walking down the block.

"Who are you?" Nicolas asked after they walked two blocks.

"I'm an old friend of Ms. Novak's."

"You look like a cop or something."

"I'm a SEAL."

Nicolas stopped in the middle of the uneven sidewalk. "For real?"

"Yep."

He blew out a breath and started walking again. "You probably think I'm scum."

"Why do you say that? Do you think I would judge you because of something your brother did? That's bullshit."

"Didn't Ms. Novak tell you I'm part of my brother's gang. I'm in *Los Demonios*. That means I'm part of something that did this. Fuck. Why didn't I see this possibility?" Kid sounded just like Aliana with the way he beat himself up.

"Hell, dude, I was part of *Las Nuevas Espadas*. I didn't get out until I was almost eighteen and joined the Navy. I wasn't responsible for everything my gang did."

"Yeah, but gangs are worse than what they were in the olden days."

This time it was Hunter who stopped walking as he barked out a laugh.

"Olden days? Jesus, Kid, just how old do you think I am?"

"Forty-five?" he asked tentatively.

"Try thirty-one. I need to start wearing a higher SPF sunscreen."

"So maybe they haven't changed much. Drugs?" Hunter nodded. "Hookers?" Hunter nodded. "Shakedowns?" Hunter nodded. "Turf-wars?"

"Oh, yeah. Somehow I managed to keep my hands clean. I never killed anyone. I dealt a little, but I stayed away from the hard stuff. I took a lot of heat for being a pussy. I was an enforcer, but mostly just intimated people because of my size."

Nicolas looked him up and down. "Yeah, I could see how that would work. But you got out. I'm going to get out. I have Ms. Novak. Most of the good ones don't have anyone like her. They don't have my opportunities, but I'm helping them."

Yep, it was just like Aliana had suspected.

"What have you been doing?"

"I've skimmed a little off some deals and got them on buses out of town. I got three of them off to different families in the Midwest through a church program. We got one girl, a working girl, into a rehab center up in the Valley. She should be getting out next week." There was such pride on the kid's face. Hell, he should be proud, but scared. Why wasn't he scared?

"Aren't you afraid of getting caught?"

"I'm doing the right thing. Ms. Novak does the right thing. She stands up to gang members at school. She expels them. She tries to make the school a bully-free environment. It doesn't work, but she tries. I'm just following in her footsteps. Plus, I read this great book," he said excitedly.

Hunter pressed the bridge of his nose. Holy fuck, if this kid was caught, they'd make an example of him for sure. He was going to be gutted.

"Let's table this for the time being."

"Okay. You want to talk about Mateo, don't you?"

"Yeah."

"Look, he didn't bomb Ms. Novak's house."

"I know he's your brother, but he attacked her. Five days before her house blew up, he attacked and cut her. It was him."

Nicolas stopped short. "So she wasn't in a car wreck, she should have told me then."

"You know that's not her," Hunter said.

"He is a dead man walking," he said in an ominous voice.

Hunter put his hand on the boy's shoulder. "Don't say things like that."

Nicolas shook off his hand. "He's a dead man," Nicolas said tightly. "What did he do to her?"

"He used a knife on her. He cut her."

"Goddammit, she's the one good thing in my life besides my mother."

"Then he bombed her house."

"No, he didn't do that," Nicolas sounded tired. "If he wanted her dead, she'd be dead. There is no way that the bomb wouldn't have worked." Nicolas raked his fingers through his curly hair. "He was trying to kill her in a way I wouldn't associate with him. But if Mateo had planted the bomb, she'd be dead for sure. He's offed at least three people, one a social worker with a bomb. There was nothing left to identify." Nicolas shuddered. "This wasn't him, he might have ordered it, but he didn't execute it."

"What are you thinking?" Hunter asked.

"Somebody wanted her to live. Somebody in Mateo's personal posse, my guess it's Rafael Lopez. He came up on me and Maria talking. I think he overheard us, but it never went anyplace. I was sweating bullets for a couple of days."

"For fuck's sake, you should have been." Hunter squeezed his shoulder. "You need to stop this happy horseshit."

"I can't. It's what I was meant to do."

"Fine, tell me about Rafael."

"I think he lives in the apartments on Eastern and Belhurst. Sometimes, he picks up some extra cash by working as a valet at a hotel downtown. It's a swanky one near the Staples Center. He gets wax impressions of car keys, so they can steal the car later, or if the guest is local and just doing a getaway weekend, he'll steal their house keys and break into their home. You should be able to find him there."

"Do you know the name of the hotel?" Hunter asked.

"It's the Blue."

Hunter nodded. He had to try again.

"Nicolas, this has got to stop."

"No. I'm on a mission." God, the kid sounded like Cesar Chavez or some shit. A real revolutionary.

"Nicolas, I understand what you're saying, but until Ms. Novak is in the clear, you need to halt all activities. She's in too much danger, and the shit you're pulling will just make her more of a target."

"You think what I've done has something to do with her house being bombed?"

"Yes, I do. Think about it. I'm guessing the kids you got out of the gang go to Bertrum High, right?"

"Yep."

"So, they'd lay that at her doorstep, wouldn't they?" The kid's eyes got wide.

"Fuck. I never considered that. I would never put her in harm's way."

"I know you wouldn't."

"Can you protect her? What should I do? How can I help?" The kid sounded fierce.

"Let's go back to the car."

"Who's the other guy?"

"He grew up around here. Now, he's really from the olden days, so you can tell him he looks fifty."

Nicolas gave him a sideways look, "I'll pass."

Yep, a smart kid.

"Zed is another Navy SEAL, I've got a third buddy who is over at her grandmother's right now watching her place."

"Is—"

"Yep, he's a SEAL, too."

"Damn, but still, unless you have all of *Las Nuevas Espadas*, I don't think you're going to be able to take down *Los Demonios*," he warned.

Zed was standing outside the car and overheard what Nicolas said, Lottie wasn't there anymore.

"We're not looking to take down your brother's gang. We're looking to keep Aliana safe. Does that mean taking your brother off the board? Yes, but we want to do this the easy way," Zed assured him.

"Prison isn't easy," Nicolas said.

"It's better than dead," Zed said harshly. "He tried to kill a woman who has been nothing but good to you. Look at her," he motioned to Aliana. She was sitting back with her head against the headrest. She looked pale. She should never have put her hair in that bun. It had probably given her a headache, then with this heat, she must be really hurting. She needed to go home.

"We also want to talk to your sister, Darla."

"Why?" Nicolas asked. It was clear he was not happy with the idea.

"Ms. Rodriguez suggested she might have helpful information," Hunter said.

"That makes no sense. She's been sick. She wouldn't have anything to say." He sounded protective.

"Nicolas, if Ms. Rodriguez thinks Darla might have something to offer, she probably has a good reason why," Aliana called out softly from the car window.

All three males looked at her.

"How far do you live from here?" Hunter asked Nicolas.

"About a mile."

"Zed, why don't you take a slow walk with Nicolas, while I drive Aliana home. I'll meet up with you in thirty minutes at Nicholas' house, we'll talk more there."

"Wanna go to the taco truck on Conroy? My treat." Zed asked the kid.

"That wouldn't be too bad." Nicholas said.

"Make it an hour," Zed said. "What's your address?" he then asked Nicolas.

The kid rattled it off, and Hunter plugged it into his phone.

He got into the driver's seat and turned to Aliana, who looked too pale for his peace of mind. He rolled up the windows and put the air conditioning on max. About four blocks from her grandmother's, she started to look around.

"Take your hair down."

"What?"

"Your hair, take it down."

He pulled in behind Dalton's truck.

"You really don't like it when I wear my hair up, do you?" Her voice was husky from sleep. It went straight to his cock.

"*Mi Cariña*, you have been fighting a headache since we visited your mother, haven't you?"

She didn't answer.

"You already told me wearing your hair up in a bun, or whatever that hairdo is, just makes your head hurt more, so take your fucking hair down. This is not about me, it's about you." Her already big blue eyes got even rounder.

"Am I Jane?"

"Is this a Tarzan reference?"

She gave a quick head bob as she pulled pins out of her hair. He could give a shit what she called him as long as she wasn't hurting. He watched as she carefully put them into a certain pocket in her purse. He wasn't surprised she was so neat and tidy.

"There, are you satisfied?"

"Not quite." He pulled her close, then pushed his fingers through the wheat, ash, and gold strands and massaged her neck and scalp. She went soft against his front and whimpered. Dalton walked up to her side of the car, peeked in the window, then walked away. Good man.

"Hunter, should you be doing this?" she almost moaned the words, her Czech accent thick.

"Making you feel good? Yes, I should always make you feel good. That's my job."

"There are things you don't know," she whispered against his chest.

"Don't start with the happy horseshit," he said softly.

His heart warmed when she giggled.

Now that she was soft, warm, and pliant, he wanted to ask her again why she had sent him away, but instead, he decided to enjoy the moment. It felt too damn good not to.

"I won't start. I just need to enjoy this moment. I need it."

"Good girl." He stroked her hair until he reached the center of her back. He did it again and again until her trembling stopped. "Do you know how big of a piece of my world you were back then?"

She looked up at him. "Your letter said I was, but after dad, I stopped believing. I wanted to believe so badly, but I stopped." She pressed her head against his chest. He could feel her tears through his white t-shirt.

"You shouldn't have, *Cariña*. It was always true. Even now, what I wrote is still true. It was just you and *Mamie* and LL. And it was you and *Mamie* who made me feel clean and good about myself. But I… But down deep, I always felt dirty. Always."

She lifted her head and stared into his eyes.

"Why? I would have remembered if you weren't clean, so it wasn't that. And you were always so good. You did good and were so nice to me. How could you ever see yourself as dirty?"

"I never told you about when I was younger. I didn't want you to think less of me. I should have known it wouldn't have mattered to you, but I was ashamed."

She cupped his cheek, her thumb tracing the crease in his cheek. "Tell me."

"*Mamie* isn't really my grandmother, did you know that? She was the neighbor lady across the hall."

"No, *mi Cariño*, I didn't know that."

Something eased at her whispered endearment.

"Tell me," she encouraged.

"I remember things when I was really young. I mean *really* young. I was probably only two. I knew who my parents were even though there were three men and three women in the apartment. There were four other children living there and a baby, too. I remember they all got food, but when I was given food, my father would slap it out of my hands. I went hungry a lot. I never understand why this man hated me."

"And your mother?"

"She got slapped or hit if she gave me food, so she just stopped. It was one of the other men who would give me food. He would yell at my father. Eventually, he left with one of the women and two of the children. Even though it wasn't as cramped in the apartment, it got worse."

"The adults each had a bedroom, all the children and the baby slept in the living room. The first time I snuck out of the apartment, I was probably four. Hell, Alia, I didn't even know my real age."

"Oh, Baby. What happened?"

She had no give for herself, but when he needed some solace, she was right there. Amazing.

"I left because I saw them take out the trash, and I remembered that there had been food on Ricki's plate. I wanted what was in that trash bag. I went outside to find it and eventually, found the dumpsters for the apartment building. They were overflowing, so I was going through the plastic bags surrounding the dumpsters when *Mamie* found me. I tried to hide from her. It took her twenty minutes to coax me out from behind the bins. To this day she says it was a miracle that she was taking out the trash at midnight."

"It wasn't safe for her, was it? Why was she?" Aliana asked.

"Her cat was sick, so she said she had to get rid of the cat litter or be killed by the stench," he said with a slight grin. "Spooky was a great cat. He lived for eight years after I moved in."

"How did you get to move in?"

Hunter thought about that awful night.

"For the next six months, on different nights, I would sneak over to *Mamie's* apartment. Things at my apartment got worse because the other family moved out. I didn't realize what was going on, but I guess my parents couldn't afford it on their own. All I know is there was a lot of screaming, yelling, and hitting. One night, Dad knocked Mom down and instead of her staying down, she crawled to the bedroom and came out with a gun. I snuck out the door just before I heard the gun go off. When I was at *Mamie's* place, I heard sirens and more shots."

"What happened when the police came and questioned you?"

"They never did."

"How is that even possible?"

"*Mamie* explained it to me years later. She used to work with the county. My mom and dad died on Friday, she called a social worker friend the following Monday. She arranged for me to become her foster child. The social worker went back and found my birth certificate."

"So, you're her foster child?"

"Oh, hell no. Never underestimate Rosa Diaz. I was adopted before I was in first grade. That woman works miracles."

Aliana's fingers sifted through the hair on the side of his head.

"Why do you think you're dirty?"

"I was eating out of the trash," he bit out. "That night I went to the dumpster? That wasn't the first time, I ate out of the trash can in the house all the damn time. I wore the same clothes weeks at a time. I stunk and didn't even know it until I started going over to *Mamie's* house."

"I understand that as a child you felt ashamed and might not have been ready to tell me, but you don't feel like that now, do you?"

He grasped her hand and brought her palm to his lips. "No. No, I don't."

"Good," she said with a fierce smile.

"So, why do you still have some of your same tapes from childhood playing in your head? Why can't I tell you you're beautiful? Why can't I tell you you're my special piece of heaven?"

She tried to pull her hand away, but he wouldn't let her.

"Hunter, let me go."

"No. Answer me."

"That was never who you were, those were just sad circumstances. And I've thrown a lot of those tapes away. I have."

Her look implored him to believe her, but he didn't. If she had, she wouldn't have such a high wall built around her heart.

"So, it's okay that I call you *mi Cielito*?" he asked.

She cringed. "You're asking me to believe lies about myself. I have a mirror. I know me. I know the *real* me. You don't Hunter. I *know* me. I'm no one's piece of heaven. Especially yours. I would just drag you down. You don't need that. You don't."

"Okay, *Cariña*, calm down. Let's go back to the moment where you were playing with my hair, I really liked that."

That stopped her short. She looked at him in confusion. Good. At least he didn't need to hear her trotting out the same old shit. He picked up her hand and placed it back on the side of his head.

"Go back to what you were doing. You were giving me comfort, remember?"

She gave a shy nod.

"Now, can I hold you?"

"You're a devious *bastardo*, you know that, don't you?" she said as she melted into his arms.

"All's fair, Cariña. All's fair."

CHAPTER NINE

Aliana was awake from her nap, looking at an email from her insurance company when her phone vibrated with a text. It was Hunter. He and Dalton were outside, he'd seen her light come on, and wondered if he could give her an update on what he'd learned. She told him to give her ten minutes, and she'd open the door for him.

By the time he knocked softly on the front door, she had cocoa and coffee on the stove along with the fixings for a ham sandwich and more of her grandmother's Marlenka honey cake.

"You got all of this done in ten minutes? Just what all do you get accomplished in a day at your job?"

"What can I get for you?" How could his words embarrass her and make her happy at the same time?

"Definitely coffee and please God say you don't make it like Beatrice Price."

"What are you talking about? She makes good coffee."

"Oh yeah, she said she made it special for us because we're sailors. Never let her make the sailor batch. It won't just put hair on your chest, it'll put hair on your palms."

She giggled. "What else do you want?"

"Load me up."

"Do you always wear a gun?" she asked. She saw the butt of it under his jacket as he sat down at the table.

"I have a permit to carry a concealed weapon. I kind of feel naked without it. It comes in handy even at the most innocent events imaginable. I'll tell you the story about a friend's wedding sometime."

"A wedding? You needed a gun at a wedding?"

"It's a long story," he said, taking the mug of coffee she offered.

"You're joking me."

"Oh, *Cariña*, I wish I was. It was a scary twenty minutes."

"Scary?"

"I hate it when women and children are involved, and this time there was a newborn."

"Are they okay?"

"We had one fatality, but not the ladies or the baby."

She went to him, and put her arm around him, resting her cheek on his silky hair. She could tell that even the one death still weighed heavy on him.

"But you saved so many." She still didn't understand how they needed guns at a wedding, but if he wasn't sharing, she wouldn't probe.

"Yeah, I guess."

She kissed the top of his head and straightened.

"How big of a sandwich?"

He looked up at her and winked. "I'm a growing boy."

"Big sandwich coming up."

When she set the plate in front of him, he raised an eyebrow. "Aren't you going to have anything?"

"I'm not hungry."

"Did you eat anything when you came in earlier?"

"No, I went to bed. I wasn't feeling well."

"When was the last time you've eaten?"

She thought about it. "I had a snack before you picked me up."

"What?"

"A banana."

"No wonder you're so slim." He got up from the table. "Do you want a mug of cocoa?"

Now that she thought about it, that sounded good. "What about a piece of cake?"

"No, that's too sweet."

"Some toast?"

She started to push up from the table. Toast sounded really good, especially with peanut butter. Peanut butter toast with hot chocolate. Heaven.

"The lady wants toast," he chuckled. "Don't you dare get up. Sit your tushie back down, I'm making it."

"I want peanut butter on my toast," she called out.

"Done."

She watched him putz around the kitchen, he was very efficient. He only had to open two cabinets to find the peanut butter and bread. He had the toast up in no time.

"Here you go," he said, placing the cocoa and toast in front of her. He sat back down beside her. Up was down, and black was white. She was being an idiot because after spending twenty minutes in the car trying to push him away, she was happy they were sitting so close, their legs were touching. She definitely needed Lottie's professional services.

She watched as he took his first bite of the sandwich.

"Avocados, this is fantastic, Alia. Do you cook?"

"Yep. Mom taught me. I make a lot of Czechoslovakian dishes, but when I was in college, I shared an apartment my senior year with a girl, and she and I experimented with a lot of Italian and good old-fashioned meat and potatoes types of food. I think we got good at it. Of course, when *Maminka* came to live with me, I started cooking Czechoslovakian again."

"Would I like that?"

"I don't know. We use a whole different spice pallet than Mexican food."

"Will you cook for me?"

"Sure, I guess."

"Great, it's a date," he smiled.

"You don't let up, do you?"

"Giving up is not an option, it's in the SEAL rule book."

She needed to change the subject.

"Tell me what you found out from Nicolas, after you dropped me off. Did you find Darla?"

This time Hunter blew out a breath. "We'll get to Darla. First, let's talk about what we found."

"How bad?"

"I've seen better, I've seen worse. He offered us both a snack, and the fridge was full. He suggested we sit down at their dining table, but Zed and I were sure if we sat in the chairs, we'd break them."

"That bad?"

"These weren't second-hand. The table and chairs had to have been picked up from the street, but there was a cheery tablecloth on the table and a chipped vase with wildflowers. Even a sunflower." Hunter grinned up at her when he mentioned that last item.

Aliana chose to ignore him. "You can tell his mom makes sure her children are dressed well for school though. That kind of thing is important to her. Even Mateo was always well dressed. Did Nicolas tell you anything about him?"

"Mateo hasn't been around much anymore. Nicolas thinks Mateo might actually marry his girlfriend because he didn't crash at their place the last few months like he used to."

"I wouldn't have thought coming home to Mama would have been Mateo's style," Aliana commented.

Hunter motioned for Aliana to eat. They munched in silence. Aliana savored her treat, she hadn't realized how hungry she'd been. Midway through her toast, Hunter got up and retrieved her empty mug and refilled it.

"Here," he said as he sat back down.

"Do you want another sandwich?" she asked.

"I'm good."

She finished her toast and cocoa. "Thank you so much. This was just what I needed."

"You don't take care of yourself."

"You sound like Lottie."

"I like your friend. Zed made a play for her this afternoon when we were asking about Nicolas. She turned him down, said she was dating Ernie. Just made him want her more. We both admired her loyalty."

She was relieved not to be talking about herself. He put his hand over hers.

"I'm glad you have a friend who worries about you. You have too much responsibility and not enough people watching out for you."

"Hardly," she dismissed. "I take care of myself just fine."

Hunter just gave her a considering look. She took advantage of it and continued.

"Let's get back to Nicolas and his living conditions. Not only does his mom keep him in clothes and food, he plays an instrument. The rent on those things isn't cheap."

"You're determined not to talk about yourself, aren't you?" Hunter sighed.

"Yes, I am," she said firmly. "Tell me about their apartment."

"Three small bedrooms, one bathroom."

"How did you find that out?"

"I said I had to use the facilities."

She should have realized that. "Go on."

"While Zed kept him talking, I peeked into the rooms. One room had two bookshelves and a pretty old computer. It was clearly Nicolas' room. The mom's room is exactly what you'd expect. Neat and tidy, a crucifix over the bed. But Darla's? It was damn near all black. Is she a goth chick?"

"She wasn't when she went to Bertrum."

"Yeah, I didn't think so. There was a family picture on the wall, and she was wearing pink. Nicolas doesn't look much like his brother or his father. It looked like it was taken two or three years ago and he was already about his father's height."

"What are you talking about? Nicolas is nowhere near Mark's size."

"Who's Mark?"

"Nicolas' father. I met him about four months ago."

"Nicolas said his father is dead. He specifically pointed to the man in the picture and said he'd died two years ago."

"Then he wasn't Nicolas' father. I met his father. He stood in the back of the auditorium when Nicolas got the Clancy Bertrum Award for his paper on Climate Change."

"Are you positive he was his dad? Then who was in the photo?" Hunter asked.

"I don't know, but there was no doubt the man I met was Nicolas' dad, he was the spitting image of him. I went up and introduced myself to him. Mark even smiled like Nicolas. It was funny, from a distance he seemed like bad news, but he was nice as can be when I talked to him. He was really proud of Nicolas. That day I told him Nicolas had a real shot at getting a scholarship to college."

"How did he respond when you told him about the scholarship?"

"He told me that I shouldn't fill his son's head full of dreams that couldn't possibly come true. I told him he needed to come to my office to discuss this because I had statistics to show him. I also wanted to go over Nicolas' records with him."

"Jesus, were you going to show him a fucking PowerPoint presentation?"

"Just a printout of one," she defended. "It doesn't matter. He told me college wasn't on the horizon for Nicolas, then I explained how I thought it was possible that with the right effort, he could get a full scholarship. I could see that Mark was getting angry, so I chose to back off. I suggested we meet the following week. I gave him my card, but he never called."

"I wonder who the guy at the apartment was?" Hunter muttered.

Aliana thought it through. Neither Darla nor Mateo looked anything like Nicolas. Nor did they have any of his acumen or personality traits.

"So, Mrs. Garcia cheated on her husband? That doesn't sound right." Aliana tried to work it through her head. She'd met Ana Garcia on multiple occasions. She was deeply religious and hard-working. She cared deeply for her children. She got up from the table and started pacing. "This is so not adding up. There is no way Ana Garcia would have cheated. I would bet my 401k."

"Okay, so she doesn't cheat. Mark's the dad. What else you got?"

"When I really think it through, I can believe she's Darla and Mateo's mom, but not Nicolas'. You saw the wedding picture, does she look like Nicolas?"

"No, they don't look alike. Are you thinking he isn't her kid? You're thinking this Mark guy gave him to Ana to raise?"

"If I have to guess, Mark's probably not more than your age."

"Great, babies having babies." Now Hunter stood up, walked over to Aliana, and looked her in the eye. "There's one more piece to this fun little puzzle, Alia."

"Shoot."

"The name of *Los Demonios* gang leader is *San Marco*."

Aliana felt her eyes go big. Was he kidding? It couldn't be, but she remembered back to the day in the office when Nicolas said he was born into the gang that it was his family. Is that what he meant. Maybe he meant someone more than just Mateo.

"God, this would explain so much."

"Sure as hell would," he agreed. "Mateo is going pretty hot and heavy trying to bring his supposed brother back into the fold, and they're using a lot more gang resources than normal."

"Hunter, I think that Nicolas knows. I think he knows that Mark, I mean *San Marco* is the leader of the gang, and he's his father."

"Come sit back down and tell me why you think that." She sat next to Hunter, their knees once again touching. Hunter grabbed her hand, smiling into her eyes. "Now tell me."

"It was something Nicolas said in my office. He said he was born into the gang that they were his family. At the time, I thought he was referring to Mateo, but now I think he might have been talking about his real dad."

"I need to track down *San Marco*, and the only way I can think to do this is to find Mateo. Nicolas thinks that Darla might know who his girlfriend is."

"Great, it's like we have to keep pulling the string—find Darla to find the girlfriend to find Mateo to find San Marco. This is crazy," Aliana huffed. "Does Nicolas have any idea when Darla is going to be home."

"Add one more person to the string. We have to find her friend Ynez. According to Nicolas, Mateo and Darla got into a big fight, and Darla's been MIA ever since. He thinks she's with Ynez. He says that Ynez is crazy, and he never knows what she's going to do next."

"Oh, for God's sake. I know her from school. She is wild. This just gets better and better."

"Alia," Hunter grabbed both of her hands. "Stay with me for a moment, okay?"

"Sure, what?"

"Did Darla have many boyfriends at school?"

She thought about it for a moment. "No, I'm pretty sure she didn't. Why are you asking?"

"It's pertinent."

"She hung out with another girl, not Ynez, a real mean girl, and they made life hell for other the weaker girls. She hated boys, that was how she ended up in juvenile detention, she attempted to stab a boy. She said he accosted her, but his buddies were there and said it was unprovoked, so she ended up locked up for eight months. But Hunter, she'd been bad news from the day she entered Bertrum. I talked to her middle school counselor, it was the same thing there. She was the school bully."

"She never dated?"

"Not to my knowledge." She said slowly. Her mouth went dry. She didn't like where this was going. Not at all. She tried to pull her hands away, but he held firm. "Hunter, what aren't you telling me?"

"Darla had two additional locks installed on her bedroom door. Both of them were broken."

Images exploded across her mind.

Broken.

Broken.

Like the lock on the bathroom stall that had been broken.

Hunter's face wavered. She couldn't breathe.

Ping, the button hit the cement.

Ping. Mateo cut another button off, his foul breath blowing in her face.

Darla fighting with her older brother.

A broken lock.

A broken girl.

"How long?" Her voice sounded far away. Tinny.

"This isn't for sure."

"Tell me, Hunter. Tell me. How long has this been going on?"

"I don't know, mi *Cariña*."

Suddenly, the toast and cocoa were roiling around in her stomach.

"But how would that be possible in such a small apartment?" Had she just asked such a stupid question? "Scratch that. Monsters always find a way."

She sat there in silence as pictures went through her mind. Dizzy, she walked out of the kitchen and went into her bedroom. She picked up her cell.

"Call Lottie Rodriguez," she said into her phone. She waited for the four longest rings imaginable.

Lottie answered, "Are you okay? Why are you calling so late, Aliana?"

"Did Darla's brother rape her?"

There was silence on the phone.

"Did he?" she asked softly.

She knew what the silence met. Tears froze in her heart. *Keep it cool.*

"When did this start, Lottie?"

"You know I won't answer that."

"I asked you a question," she said politely.

She was met by silence.

"When did this start?"

She remembered the first time she pulled the girl into her office, the thick eyeliner, the bright red lipstick that went with the sneer. The foul language. "Was it happening that first time I wrote her up?"

"Aliana—"

"Tell me!" she shouted.

Warm arms circled her. She didn't want that. She didn't deserve that.

"You didn't know, Honey. You couldn't know," Lottie said softly.

"I was tormenting this girl when she was being abused. I was adding to her abuse."

Lottie was silent. "You didn't know, Honey. You would never knowingly hurt anyone."

She felt a tear fall. She dropped the phone on the bed. Hunter picked up the phone and said something, she didn't know what. She was lost in her own head. Remembering every fucking time she had run into that girl in the hall. Every single time she'd told her to straighten up, or that she was watching her.

She didn't even realize she was crying until Hunter pulled her into his arms.

"Ah, Cariña, you're breaking my heart."

She pictured Darla and that evil, twisted, sick brother of hers forcing her to have sex. He was a demon. He needed to die.

How many other children had she misjudged over the years?

"Aliana, talk to me."

She couldn't. "Hold me."

"Always." She burrowed closer. He'd always been her talisman.

"Láska?" her grandmother asked from the doorway. Aliana looked up from Hunter's arms. Babička was in her robe. "What happened?"

"I'm fine. I just heard some bad news about one of my students. It happened a long time ago." She cleared her throat and swiped at some of her tears. "Go back to bed."

"Do you want me to make you some cocoa?"

Aliana gave a weak laugh. "I already had some Babička. I'll be fine."

"Hunter, do you have her?" her grandmother asked.

"Yes. She just had a shock. I'll take care of her," he promised as his arms gently tightened. Even now, he was careful of her bruises. "I'm going to get her to bed soon. She still has to meet the book club tomorrow."

"She should have warm milk now, anyway, the chocolate would keep her up. You'll make that for her?"

"I will. I promise."

"Good night, then."

Hunter didn't move. He just stood there holding her. She took comfort even though she knew it was wrong. Eventually, enough was enough.

"Let's go back to the kitchen?"

"Are you sure?" he asked.

"Yeah. After all, this isn't about me, this is about Darla. I had no reason to be crying. I need to think of a way to be helping her, not in my bedroom having a pity party. That's ridiculous."

"Alia, you're one of the most empathetic people I know. Of course, this would hit you hard."

She closed her eyes. She pictured the broken locks, then pushed it away.

"Hunter, let's finish this." She pushed out of his arms and headed to the kitchen. She picked up the dishes from the table and they clattered as she shoved them into the sink.

"Alia?"

"We have to figure out where Darla is. We need to make sure she's safe."

"We'll do that, *Cariña*, I promise."

"You need to find that fucker, Mateo and crush him."

"That was already on the agenda." He coaxed her back to the table. "We're going to use Nicolas to accomplish both of those things. He's already given us a lead."

"I don't want you to use Nicolas. He's innocent."

"No, he's not, *mi Cielieto*, he's a member of *Los Demonios*, and don't you forget it."

"I know that," she dismissed. "But he told you what he's doing. He's trying to get people to quit. He's quietly recruiting people out of the gang. And what are you acting all high and mighty about? You and Zed were gang members too."

"Right. Don't canonize any of us. We all have feet made of clay."

"Hunter, I don't have any of you up on a pedestal, but I can be pretty damned impressed by all of you. Well, except for Zed, I don't think he likes me. But you and Nicolas are remarkable."

Hunter got an odd expression on his face, then picked up her hand, brought it to his mouth and kissed her palm.

"What was that for?" She was dazed.

"For seeing me as who I am." He paused and cupped the back of her neck. "I see you too. I do. I think you're a remarkable woman, and I'm blessed to have you in my life."

Her throat was tight. She couldn't respond.

He brought her forward and did the most astounding thing. His lips touched hers. She kept her eyes wide open, staring at him, watching as his eyes closed. His other hand came up and cupped her cheek and his lips feathered over her lips, coaxing. Coaxing what? She felt a tingle, a warmth spreading as she followed his lead. She was no longer looking at him. Her hands were gripping his shoulders, and his mouth settled softly on hers, guiding her slowly into a haze of wonder.

She started when she felt his tongue trace her bottom lip, but then the soft caress beguiled her into opening her mouth. Their breath mingled as he deepened their kiss. Oh God, she was kissing Hunter, and it was beautiful. The thought flew away as the tip of his tongue touched hers. She heard a whimper. His big hand moved down to her throat, his thumb sliding over her pulse. He did it again and again as if to calm her, but how could she calm down when his tongue was sliding against hers? She held onto his shoulders for dear life. In the distance, she heard more sounds. Gradually his mouth lifted from hers, and he kissed the side of her mouth, her cheek and then her closed eyelids.

"Are you okay?" he asked softly.

"Oh yes."

"You were whimpering."

So that was what that sound was. She opened her eyes. His eyes were dark and mysterious, it was like he held the secrets of the world. No. It was like he held the secrets of *her* world.

"Can you do me a favor?" he asked quietly.

"I'll try."

"Tell me why you asked me to leave you. Tell me what happened the night your dad died."

She felt like he slipped a knife into her. Had he kissed her to soften her up so she would tell him?

He traced her pulse point again, and she realized he still held her.

"This isn't an ambush, *Cariña*. That kiss was a decade too long in coming. Tell me. Make me understand."

* * *

Hunter watched this woman, who meant so much to him, go from warm with desire to wounded. He hated that, but he had to do it. This might be his one and only opportunity to get to the bottom of things while she was this vulnerable. It was past time, thirteen years pastime, that he found out why she had thrown them away.

"*Cariña*, talk to me." He drew his thumb upward and brushed her bottom lip where she was biting it. He'd kept his kiss as soft and gentle as he could because even now, her bottom lip was slightly swollen from the explosion. He knew from her reaction, she'd enjoyed it. He also guessed his Alia hadn't been kissed much. There was too much surprise and wonder in her responses. His heart ached for her.

"Can you hold me? Like you did under the bleachers?" her voice was so soft, he could barely hear her words. Her nails were still biting into his shoulders.

"Always." He led her into the other room and settled them on the couch. She sat away from him.

"Hunter, I've tried to work it out in my mind. I've dug out some of the rot, I have, but some of it is rooted so deep, it'll never come free." She dug her fists into her thighs, her mouth set in a grimace.

"God knows, I've needed help with shit before. You helped me earlier, just listening about meeting *Mamie* at the dumpster."

She gave him a considering look, then a small smile. "God knows, I want my shit gone, too."

"Come here," he said. Hunter opened his arms. His heart about burst in his chest the way she burrowed into him. He wrapped both arms around her.

"My *Táto* seemed happy when I was young. Before he'd been forced to leave Czechoslovakia and move to America, he'd been a professor of literature and poetry at the University," she said with pride.

Hunter shook his head. He was impatient to hear about his suicide, but she needed to get this out in her own way.

"He taught me how to write poetry. His poems were so stark, full of beauty and love."

"Like your songs, I bet."

"My songs don't even come close to *Táto's* poems. He had two books of poetry published back in the old country. I still have them." She sounded both proud and sad.

"He sounds very accomplished. What did he do here in the United States?"

"He loved the Czech language so much, he didn't want to learn English. He resented having to flee Czechoslovakia even though it wasn't safe for him there."

"What did he do for a living here?" he asked again.

"He worked in the foundry for my grandfather. That's how he met my mother."

"Oh, yeah, I knew he worked there." A picture of a blonde man came to mind, he had always seemed out of place in his work boots and overalls.

"I didn't realize how much this bothered him until I was in the seventh grade. I wrote two poems for English class, and the teacher had them put in the school newspaper. I was so excited. Of course, Heather made fun of me, but for once, that didn't matter. Some of the other kids complimented me."

"I remember when that happened. I walked you home that day." She had been so excited, she had practically danced beside him down the sidewalk.

"When I presented *Táto* the school paper, he hardly said a word. I showed him how I had used imagery just like he'd taught me, but he walked away." Aliana's voice was quiet as she told her story, her accent thick like it had been in childhood. "At dinner, *Maminka* asked me to translate one of the poems into Czech, but it didn't sound right. The rhymes and rhythms were off. *Táto* had me read, then repeat them again in English, but I could tell he was getting frustrated when he didn't understand all the words. He got up from the dinner table and went to bed. *Táto* didn't eat dinner with us for three nights in a row, he said he had headaches after work. I thought I had disappointed him. Eventually, I realized that was the turning point."

"What do you mean?"

"Before that, *Táto* always held on to some sort of dream that he would go home to Czechoslovakia, or maybe our block would turn into Little Prague, and he would be mayor. Somehow, he would get to relive his old glory, but that day, when he saw me somewhat acclimated to America, that killed it for him. Something went wrong. His dreams started to slowly die, and it was *Maminka* and my fault." She shivered, Hunter rubbed her arms, and she huddled closer.

"I could have handled it. I was used to people hating me for some unwarranted offense. *Maminka* had gone from being the apple of her parent's eyes to living with my father. She adored him, and the more he pushed her away or resented her, the harder she tried to be perfect." Her voice trailed off.

Hunter knew as much as she said she could handle it, Aliana would have been just as hurt as her mother. His little

Alia always tried to be perfect for everyone, and everyone stomped on her.

"Tell me."

"My mom was eighteen when she married my dad. She went straight from her father's house to a little apartment her husband provided. There was only ever one car, so there was no need for her to drive. I remember when I was twelve, for no reason at all, *Táko* got mad at Mom because she couldn't drive to the big warehouse store across town—she always walked or took the bus most places—I thought he was going to hit her. She didn't cry, she just apologized for weeks. Her dad was dead, so she had her mom teach her to drive."

"He didn't teach her?"

"That night, he said she was an anchor, that he had to do everything, that she was nothing but another responsibility hanging around his neck, just like I was. She was too scared to ask him."

Hunter felt the hair on the back of his neck rise. He remembered her saying she was relieving him of all responsibility. Was this what it went back to?

Hunter didn't bother asking stupid questions, like why a man would think something like that. As far as he was concerned, her father should have kissed the ground his wife and daughter walked on. He was the problem, never bothering to acclimate, spending his time bemoaning the life he had lost, instead of cherishing the gifts he'd been given.

"So, he was a selfish bastard," Hunter bit off.

"Not always. *Maminka* showed me the yearbooks of the university where he taught. He was praised by all of his students and was constantly going above and beyond. Occasionally, I think I'm like him," she gave a sad laugh. "Pretty scary, huh?"

"You're nothing like him." Hunter hugged her fiercely. She clutched him back just as tightly. He waited until her breathing evened out.

"Tell me about the day he killed himself."

She flinched against him.

"I'm sorry, *mi Cielieto*, I didn't mean to scare you."

"You didn't, I just… I just…" She brought her feet up on the couch, her knees to her chest. It was almost the same pose she'd had under the bleachers those many years ago. He wrapped both arms around her, and she tugged them tighter and buried her face in the crook of his arm.

"I got out of school early, it was parent-teacher conference day. When I got home, the door to the apartment was unlocked. I called out to see who was home. *Táto* came out of the bedroom and said *Maminka* was over at *Babička's* house making jam. He went back into his room, but he left the door open. I needed to talk to him. I thought he was home because he knew someone had to go meet with my teachers."

Hunter could barely understand her. It wasn't her beautiful accent, it was that her voice was thick with tears.

"I'm right here. You're in my arms. You can tell me anything, and you're safe, right here in my arms. I have you, Alia, you're safe," he said over and over again as he stroked her hair.

Aliana seemed to go inward. He waited, letting her tell the story in her own time, her own way.

* * *

Aliana had never shared this. Not even with the psychiatrist she'd seen in college who had helped her with so much. But here, in the safety of Hunter's arms, she could bring the nightmare out into the light.

Her parents' room was dim, the curtains were drawn. It smelled of roses. It was her mother's favorite scent. Her dad stood out, sitting on the flowered bedspread in his overalls.

"Papa? Are you home to go to meet with my teachers?" she asked in Czech as she stepped into the room. A sliver of sunlight escaped the drapes and hit the barrel of the gun in her father's hand. He had it pointed upwards at himself. He was staring down at it. The blue-black steel looked evil. Now that she saw it, she couldn't take her eyes off it.

"What do you need now? What is it this time that I have to do for you? It's always about you and your mom. What would you have me do?" he sneered.

Aliana heard him, but she couldn't answer. His thumb traced the tip of the gun, the cloying smell of roses was assaulting her nose.

"Answer me!"

She jumped and stumbled further into the room.

"Look at you, you can't even keep your feet. You whine about being made fun of, but you're clumsy."

"Why do you have a gun?"

"Protection. In this neighborhood, we need protection." As he waved the gun, her head moved with it as if charmed by a snake. "Do you want to see it?"

"No."

"Come here."

She stayed glued to the carpet. This man wasn't her Papa.

"Why are you home from school, Girl?"

"It's parent, teacher conference day. You need to go talk to my teachers," she said, then swallowed, praying he wouldn't yell at her or worse.

"Just another goddamn thing that you need. What about what I need? Do you know what happened today? I left the foundry. We parted ways. Seventeen years and that new supervisor thinks he knows more than I do?" Her dad spit on the floor. "He knows nothing. Nobody knows anything."

Aliana stared at her father. She had visited the foundry so often when her grandfather had been alive. It was a magical place, but she knew her father hated it, he never said so, but she could tell. He wanted to go back to the university in Czechoslovakia, he wanted to relive his glory.

"Do you know why I stayed?" he asked her.

He turned the gun over in his hands. He rolled it over. First, it pointed at him. Then it pointed at her. Sweat popped out on her brow, and fear made her teeth clench. She couldn't speak, so she shook her head.

"Answer me. Do you know why I stayed at that goddamn job?"

"No, Papa, why?"

"Because of you and your mom. All either of you has ever been is a responsibility that has weighed me down. You flushed my dreams down the toilet, the two of you."

"Mama loves you. I love you."

"That's the worst lie of all, saying you love me. You and your mom tied a rope around my neck and pulled me under water too many times. Your type of love kills, Aliana. It kills."

Dread filled her as he lifted the gun. At that moment, she had no idea if he was going to shoot her. But if he did, it would have been fine. His words felt like death.

"Did you run?" Hunter asked.

"Yes, I ran toward him. I was afraid he would shoot himself, I wanted to stop him."

"Fuck, Alia." He gripped her so tight, it hurt, but she made no sound, she was lost in those hellishly long minutes in the past.

Her father shoved the barrel of the gun into his chin. His doughy flesh gobbled up the steel.

"Don't!" she screamed as she lunged. The sound of the shot burst through her brain. She couldn't hear anything. She watched the gun fall to the floor, but didn't hear it thud. Her father fell sideways on the bed, a rich river of red poured from her father's cheek and throat. She mashed her hands on both, trying to stem the tide.

His eyes were open, she saw life. She begged him not to die. "Please Papa, live. I love you so much. Live. I love you." She pulled up the bedspread and pushed it into the wound, but the blood saturated the blanket like water from a faucet.

"Papa, can you hear me? Live." She couldn't even hear her

own words because her ears were still ringing from the sound of the gun going off. She watched as life faded from his blue eyes.

"No! Don't go," she screamed and pleaded. She didn't know how long she stayed like that, sobbing and pleading. The old neighbor next door, he came, then the police. Finally, her mother. She didn't remember much. Her one clear thought was to never tell her mother what her father had said. Never tell anyone. Never ever.

Everyone thought Laszlo Novak committed suicide because he lost his job, and she did everything in her power to perpetuate that myth. She never told anyone until now that it was because of her and her mom.

"That's bullshit, Alia," Hunter roared in a soft, fierce whisper.

She had forgotten where she was or that she was with Hunter.

"Do you hear me? I'll yell loud enough so your grandmother wakes up, and Dalton comes running, I don't care. What he said was wrong. It's wrong, *mi Amor*. Wrong."

She took her face out of its hiding place in order to look at Hunter, he looked like he had been tortured. Why?

She slipped into Spanish, "Darling, don't worry. I've made peace with this. I coped. I did the right things. I made sure my mom never knew what he said. She loved him so much, and it would have shattered her world."

"So, you kept this buried inside you, eating away like acid? You said you didn't even tell your shrink. What the fuck, Alia? Why not?"

She cringed at his words, and for the first time, being in his arms didn't feel good. She tried to get up.

"No, you're not going anywhere. This time, I'm not letting you get away, you hear me? I get it now. I get why you sent me away all those years ago, and it breaks my fucking heart. All those years, Alia. All those lost years. Do you know what we could have been to one another?" Was he saying what she thought he was? It wasn't possible. She stopped moving and stared up into his eyes.

"You were meant for better things," she whispered.

"Better than what?"

"Better than me. I would have done to you what my mother did to my father. What *I* did to my father."

"Your dad was a headcase. A cruel one, at that."

She flinched. "I'm a headcase too, didn't you hear, I had a shrink in college?" She winced as soon as she heard the words come out of her mouth. She knew better than that. Apparently, so did Hunter because he didn't let it slide.

"That just tells me you had the good sense to get help. Do you know I've had to go to the military shrink? Our missions can really mess with our heads. Sometimes, we need help to keep it together. Off the top of my head, I can think of one man, who I really respect, who had to spend over a year on a couch, probably needed meds too. He had to really fight his way back. He wasn't a headcase, he *is* a hero."

She let out a long trembling sigh. "This is a lot."

"I imagine it is. Jesus, that's a fuckload of poison you've been holding onto."

"I think I feel a bit better," she admitted.

"Baby, while you try to sort that out, can I hold you? I'm scared to let you go."

She looked at him questioningly.

In a display of strength that astounded her, he picked her up, while reclining on the couch. Then he laid her on top of himself. He snagged the afghan from the back of the sofa and draped it over her.

"Will you be comfortable if we sleep like this tonight? I'm afraid if I leave, you'll disappear behind a wall again."

She relaxed into the heat of his body, stretching and arranging herself until she fit comfortably.

"You're killing me," he whispered huskily.

"What?"

"Never mind, *Chaquita*. I think we're going to have to work our way up to some things. Something tells me my Alia is a little naïve."

"I am not," she protested hotly as she pushed up on his chest to look into his eyes. "I'm a Vice Principal of a school. I know lots of things."

"Been kissed much?" he asked.

She dropped her forehead to his chest and whispered, "No."

"Go to sleep, *mi Cielieto*. I have you."

She yawned. She was absolutely drained. She hadn't thought she would be able to sleep on top of Hunter, but the last thing she heard was the beating of his heart.

CHAPTER TEN

Hunter got a text from Dalton at one a.m.

"*Cariña*, I need to go." He was blanketed by blonde hair, the stuff of dreams.

"Mmmmm?" She woke up languid and sweet. "You're so warm," she said in a husky whisper, burrowing closer.

His hands enveloped her small back. She needed to eat more, it was probably why she was cold. He would see to it.

"I'll be back later to take you to *Mamie's*."

"It's Saturday already?"

He looked up and saw the bruising on the left side of her face was turning yellow. He trailed his fingers against it. Brushed his thumb across her bottom lip. Just one, he promised himself. His lips touched hers, and she flowered open.

He molded their lips together and was rewarded when he felt her nipples prod his chest. He shifted, and she moaned and twisted against him. He drew back and began seducing her mouth with licking, nipping, and nibbling kisses until she grabbed his ears and pressed her lips against his, thrusting her tongue into his mouth.

He had never been so tempted by a kiss. His hand went to the back of her neck, and he tilted her head so he could get a better angle to feast. Her silken tongue lured him to new heights, her soft heat driving him crazy. He hooked one hand around her thigh and drew it around his, so she was straddling him, his cock cradled by her jean-clad heat. Her hands moved from his ears to his face, down to his shoulders, and he felt her fingers bite. It was the only thing that penetrated his haze of desire.

His woman's body was sliding slowly, sensuously, innocently against his. He smoothed back the glory of her hair, hating to do so. It was as if he was bringing in the outside world when he lifted back the veil of sunshine.

"Easy, *mi Amor*," he brushed a tender kiss against her temple.

She took a deep breath. Then another. And then…and then…she smiled.

"Hunter."

"Yes?"

"No, just Hunter. I've said your name so often in my head when I needed strength when I needed joy when I needed saving. And now you're here."

Her words hit him in the heart.

His phone vibrated. It wasn't a text this time, it was a call. Aliana recognized it and sat up, pulling the afghan around herself.

"Yeah?" he said into the phone.

"Zed's got a situation. If you don't get your ass out of the house now, I'm taking your bike and going. He needs some backup. He thinks he has a lock on Ynez and Darla, and it's not good." Hunter was up off the couch and putting on his boots before Dalton finished his last sentence.

"Gotta go, *Cariña*. Lock up behind me."

"Hunter, what's—"

"Gotta go." He snagged his shoulder holster and jacket and flew out the door sure Aliana would follow his orders. He plugged in the tracking program on Zed in his phone. Dalton and Hunter had added him to their network first thing.

"Fuck," he said to Dalton as he got to his bike.

"What?"

"The girls are in the middle of *Las Nuevas Espadas* territory. No wonder Zed is calling in backup."

"How bad is that?"

"They're *Los Demonios*, it's not so much the men of the gang as the women of the *Espadas*. Not good at all," Hunter said as he swung his leg over his bike. He pressed a number into his phone.

"Hey LL, need a favor, my man."

"You always need favors."

"Yeah, well, it's Friday night, and I don't have any information on Mateo, now do I? So, since you haven't delivered on that one, maybe this one you *can* deliver on."

"You're trying my patience."

Hunter took a calming breath.

"LL, there are two girls, both of them high school age, one of them is four months pregnant. They're in your territory, and they're in trouble. I don't have the details, but I have a friend monitoring the situation, and he wants me over ten minutes ago, so I know it's bad. I need you to intervene."

"These girls are with *Los Demonios*?"

"Yeah, they're over at the club on Seturnas and Lennox. They're in line, waiting to get into the club."

"I'll send Martin, he's the closest."

"A friend of mine, Zed, he'll be there. Can't miss him, my size. Half Mexican. When things escalate, he's stepping in."

"Got it. I'll tell Martin. Is he a SEAL?"

"Affirmative."

LL laughed. "I love that shit."

Hunter hung up the phone on LL's laughter.

He shoved his phone deep into his jacket's inner pocket and strapped on his helmet. He gave a low wave to Dalton and rode out toward *Las Nuevas Espadas* territory.

Fifteen minutes later, he heard the sound of gunfire as he turned a corner onto the Lennox. He came to a halt because young men and women, mostly teenagers dressed to the hilt, ran past him. They were on the sidewalk and the street, yelling and screaming in fear. One girl literally fell into his bike, then righted herself, leaving a high heel, and scrambled behind him to continue on. He heard more gunshots. The only solace he could take is it wasn't an automatic weapon.

He put down his bike and pushed against the crowd toward the club. He sprinted over the downed red velvet rope and jumped over the gold stanchions. At the entrance of the dark club, he pulled out his gun and ducked inside.

His eyes acclimated quickly as he slid against the wall. He saw the hostess stand and a curtain behind it. Screams pierced the air. He heard more gunshots and then a deafening explosion of glass crashing. He peeked through the curtain and saw dim, ambient lighting, spreading prisms of color from a shattered chandelier that showered the dance floor. He saw multiple bodies lying in the midst of the debris, one trying to get up. Were they stupid?

To the right was a bar which encompassed nearly the entire wall. The mirror was also in pieces as were most of the bottles of booze. He saw two muzzle flashes in rapid succession come from the top of the bar. Somebody must be firing blind.

"Get down," Zed said as he ran across the dance floor and shoved the girl who was trying to get up back to the floor. He zigzagged as he flew toward the bar, shooting his weapon.

"Got you covered," Hunter yelled. He saw another flash from the other end of the bar, but this shooter stood up. Hunter took aim and hit his target in the head. He searched the room for other bogeys as Zed jumped the bar.

On the floor, he saw someone struggling to lift their arm. Was that a weapon? He couldn't tell. He felt the glass splinter beneath his boots as he ran to the figure who was raising their hand. He stomped on their arm, and felt it break, the woman screamed as the gun dropped from her useless fingers.

The stream of curses was long and colorful as Hunter raised his boot. He looked around to the others on the dance floor. He counted seven, five women and two men, teenagers really. One was dead, her head crushed from one of the arms of the huge chandelier. A boy was helping a girl sit up. A girl lying on top of another girl suddenly moved.

"Whore!" she screamed in Spanish. She punched the girl underneath her. Hunter moved forward and pulled her off the unconscious girl. When he did, he found Darla. He recognized her from the picture at Nicolas' apartment.

"Darla! Is she alright?" Another girl crawled over, uncaring of the glass.

"Are you Ynez?" Hunter asked.

"Yeah."

He heard sirens. They didn't have much time. He felt for Darla's pulse. It was strong. He felt along her body, noting the slight swell of her abdomen, she didn't appear to have any broken bones. She moaned.

"Ynez?"

"I'm here, Darla."

"Bitch came at me from behind," Darla snarled.

"Her man pulled a gun on the guy you were dancing with," Ynez said.

"Yo! Tex! We gotta get outta here, you find your girls?"

Hunter heard Martin's shout from the front of the club.

"We need an ambulance, Martin," Hunter yelled. "Zed, what's your status?"

"I'm good," Zed said in a normal voice. Hunter looked up. He was right behind him. He crouched down beside Hunter. "Darla, we're friends of your brother, Nicolas. We're going to get you some help," Zed said in Spanish.

"Sure you are," she said bitterly.

"We are," Hunter reiterated. "Mateo's a thing of the past. He won't be coming back to bother you ever again."

"Bullshit."

"But first we need to know where he is."

She didn't say a word. She rolled to her side, hugging her abdomen.

"Can you really make sure that bastard gets what's coming to him?" Ynez asked.

"Absolutely," Hunter answered.

She gave him a long, considering look in the darkened club. "Mateo's slut girlfriend is set up in a nice place over on Olympic Blvd. It's called Fern Terrace, the same apartment where the singer Polly lived before she was discovered. Mateo's bitch thinks she can sing, but she's got nothing but fake tits."

"What's her name?"

"Huh?"

"Name. What's her name?" Zed demanded.

"We've gotta go!" Martin shouted. "Cops are a block away."

"The bitch is Juanita, don't know her last name. But she dyes her hair red. She looks ridiculous."

"Got it," Zed said.

"Ynez, stay with Darla," Hunter said. "She's going to need to go to the hospital. Tell Nicolas where she's at. We'll find her and tell her when it's safe to go home."

"You get that motherfucker. Make sure he dies bad."

"Shut up, Ynez. You promised not to tell." Darla started to cough.

"We'll take care of this." Hunter got to his feet and so did Zed. Hunter took one last look at the girl who couldn't be much bigger than a minute, except for her bulging belly. Yep, Mateo already had his head on the chopping block, but now his method of dying just got uglier.

* * *

Aliana watched her grandmother's eyes gleam as she brought in her kozunak sweet bread. Hunter had mentioned yesterday that Velma was baking a German chocolate cake, so Babička was pulling out all the stops at today's book club. Then she noticed the dining room table where *Mamie* indicated her grandmother put her dessert. It was loaded for bear. Aliana smothered a laugh. Apparently, the ladies were in a competition to spoil Hunter. She hoped he was hungry.

"Son?" A woman with a cane walked up to Hunter and poked him in the belly with the point of her cane. Hunter kept a straight face.

"Yes, ma'am. What can I do for you?"

"Do you have your VA card?" Her wrist got shaky, so Hunter gently lowered her cane to the ground and smiled at her.

"I don't think we've been properly introduced. I'm Petty Officer First Class, Hunter Diaz. I'm active service, so I don't need a VA card." He helped her sit down on the couch next to Aliana's grandmother.

"Well, you better get one. They are invaluable. Saved my grandson, Walter, on one of them there iPhones. He also got free online tutoring, which he desperately needed, all because of that there card."

"It's for Veterans ma'am, I'm active duty," Hunter explained again.

"And you get a discount on your underwear. The next time I see you, you better have your card."

Hunter sighed, "Yes, ma'am." He turned away from her and Aliana smothered a grin when she saw him get poked again by the cane.

"He got really good insurance too."

"The VA card is really important to get. I know, I'll tell all my veteran buddies to arrange for one the day they get out."

"You're a good boy," she smiled. "Now go get me a brownie and some lemonade."

Aliana couldn't hold it in. She laughed outright as Hunter went over to the dessert table. Mrs. Diaz stood up in the middle of the room.

"Ida is the only one who couldn't make it," she said to the assembled group. "I know we were all excited to discuss Lori King's latest release, especially that one scene," *Mamie* fanned herself, and the women laughed.

Velma looked over at Hunter as he bent over to deliver the brownies and gave him an appraising look. "Too bad we couldn't have your grandson reenact a scene."

Mrs. Diaz got a sour look on her face. "Really Velma, that's taking things just a little too far, don't you think?"

Aliana snuck a peek over at her grandmother, and she was whispering with the 'cane' lady. Aliana now knew that blushing was a hereditary trait.

"I'm sorry, Rosa," Velma said, a definite twinkle in her eye. "Now, I'd like to go first. I've been doing some checking. I talked to Father Michael at St. Anthony's, and he suggested I talk to Sister Xena over at the Mission First Street Mission. She told me about Hank the homeless man who hangs out over on—"

"Velma, please, for God's sake, get to the point already," Mrs. Diaz sighed.

"I'm just trying to tell you I definitely spent some time investigating this."

"We all got the picture."

Aliana glanced over at Hunter, who was rubbing his mouth, obviously trying to smother a grin.

Velma leaned forward. "Word on the street is *Los Demonios* is losing members and not because they're being recruited by other gangs, they're disappearing."

Aliana's shoulders slumped. After the big buildup, she'd really been hoping for new information.

"Velma, we knew that," Rosa said sharply. "I told all of you that on the phone."

"Well, there's more." She lowered her voice. "All of them were either currently attending Bertrum or had gone there at one time. That's why you were targeted, Aliana. And—"

A tiny woman sitting in the corner eating some a plate of sweet bread snorted. "How in the fuck can that be Aliana's fault? Everyone knows *Los Demonios* pretty much came from Bertrum High and *Las Nuevas Espadas* come from Lincoln High."

Aliana shuddered at the name of her old alma mater. She hated that school.

"Esther, you agreed not to drop the F-Bomb today," said a woman in a pretty pink sweater set. Her low Cuban heels, lipstick, and hair matched her suit. Aliana would bet anything she was the one who brought the pink cupcakes.

"He's a sailor, he's heard the word fuck before," Esther said before popping another piece of bread into her mouth.

"You're not listening to me," Velma raised her voice.

"What?" Rosa Diaz asked.

"I was trying to tell you that San Marcos lost three of his prostitutes last week. He thought they were recruited by *Las Nuevas Espadas*, but I found out from my beautician's cousin who is a friend of—"

"We don't care how you found out. Just tell us the information," Esther growled.

"Two days ago, he was able to track their last known whereabouts to Union Station. He wants those girls back, and he's positive Aliana knows where they are."

"But I don't," she protested. But she would bet anything that Nicolas did. Hunter reached over and grabbed her hand in his.

"That is really good work, Velma," he smiled. The woman preened under his praise.

"Does anyone else have anything to add?" Rosa Diaz asked.

"I found this book a little too racy, perhaps we can choose something more appropriate next time. Something without a half-naked man on the cover?" The woman in the pink suit said. "I found this book with a man in a suit on the cover. It's called 'Fifty Shades of Gray', maybe we could read that instead before our next meeting."

Esther's eyes began to water, and she started coughing.

Velma spoke up. "Florence, there is no way we're not going to finish our discussion of Lori's new book."

Esther finally caught her breath. "But, Honey, after that, Fifty Shade's of Gray would be a wonderful pick."

CHAPTER ELEVEN

"That Esther woman is just evil," Aliana laughed as Hunter opened the door to her hybrid.

Hunter put the two bags of food in the backseat next to Mrs. J. He wasn't in the mood to laugh. He took out his cell phone and texted Dalton to call him. He'd had enough downtime as far as he was concerned. They needed to find a safe house for the women, stat.

"This isn't the way home," Aliana's grandmother noted.

"Nope, it isn't. We're going to a hotel."

"No, we're not Hunter Diaz," she said in an awfully firm voice for such an elderly woman. "We're going to my house."

"San Marcos knows where you live. Did you not hear that he wants to take Aliana and ask her questions?"

"I did. But you're going to protect her. You and your friends have been doing a beautiful job so far. Please continue to do so."

He'd take them somewhere near Shorinda's house, that way they could visit Danica. It would be perfect. His phone rang.

"What's up?" Dalton asked.

"The leader of *Los Demonios* has upped his game. Apparently, our boy Nicolas has liberated three prostitutes, and San Marcos is laying the blame at Aliana's feet. He wants the girls back, and he plans to bring her in to question her. I need a hotel to stash her and her grandmother, preferably near Shorinda's house. Find one."

"On it." Dalton hung up.

"Hunter, how bad is this? I mean you can't take on the entire gang. It was one thing when it was just Mateo, but now it is the leader of one of the biggest Mexican gangs in East L.A." He heard the tremble in her voice.

He grabbed her hand and rubbed his thumb along her knuckles. "You're going to be fine."

"It's not me I'm worried about."

"So is your mom and grandmother."

"You're not hearing me," she whispered fiercely. "You came here thinking you could protect me, and maybe help me fight off some lowlife, but this is crazy. You can't take them on. Nobody can."

He continued driving, trying to avoid the numerous potholes on the major street that would take them up to Glendale.

"I admit, this has become a bit more of a problem than I anticipated."

"Exactly. This is a move to a different state problem."

Hunter laughed. "*Cariña*, this just requires a small adjustment of plans."

"Don't laugh," she looked over her shoulder at her grandmother. He looked in the rearview mirror and saw that Mrs. J's eyes were drooping. Aliana glanced back at him. "Take me to the police station right now."

"And tell them what? That Velma's beautician's cousin's aunt's podiatrist told her that some prostitutes left town, and now you're a target of *Los Demonios*?"

"Yes," she hissed.

"Yeah, that'll go over well. I'm sure they'll be Johnny on the spot to offer you protection."

"My house blew up. I still haven't told them all they wanted to know about that. So, if I'm honest about that, then…" her voice trailed off.

"Then they'll take Nicolas into custody," he finished for her.

She grabbed his hand with both of hers. "I've got to take Maminka and Babička and move out-of-state."

"There isn't a chance in hell you're moving out-of-state. San Marcos is going down. And so is Mateo," he said with grim satisfaction.

He thought about the teenager who had been lying on the dance floor last night. Lottie had called them from the hospital this morning to say she and the baby were doing fine. He needed one more player. Preferably someone who had been through the fire and wasn't afraid to get his hands dirty. He knew just the man.

* * *

Aliana could hear Nat King Cole singing 'Rambling Rose' as they walked up the walkway to Shorinda's modest house.

"Oh no," her grandmother said.

Aliana ran to the door and pounded.

"What is it *Cariña?*" Hunter called from beside her grandmother.

She didn't hear what *Babička* told him because Shorinda opened the door, her dark face, stricken.

"Come in, Girlfriend." She looked over Aliana's shoulder. "Oh, thank God, she's been calling for her *Maminka* for hours. You haven't been answering your cell phone."

Sakra, she'd had it on Do Not Disturb. Hunter and *Babička* came up behind her. She could now hear her mother shouts.

"My baby," her grandmother said in Czech. She pushed past Shorinda and headed down the hallway.

"What happened?" Aliana asked Shorinda.

"She woke up like this about four hours ago. Unfortunately, her blood pressure is too low to administer a sedative or Valium. I've been playing some of her favorite music. There are certain antipsychotics that could be administered, but I didn't bring any. I'm sorry, I effed up."

"Has this ever happened back at the facility?" Aliana asked the worried nurse.

"No."

"Then how could you have predicted it?"

The music stopped, then the yelling stopped, and Aliana heard her grandmother singing. Shorinda sagged with relief. She sat down on the couch.

"Thank you, baby Jesus."

Aliana smiled slightly when she saw Hunter's smile.

"Have you eaten today?" Aliana asked Shorinda.

"No, neither has your mom."

"Well, we certainly have dessert covered," Hunter said. "Let me bring that in."

"I'm going to see what you have in the kitchen. I can make us something for lunch."

"I planned to make fried chicken."

Aliana laughed at Hunter's hopeful expression. "Shorinda, you just sit and rest. I've got that covered. Hunter why don't you call Dalton and Zed and see if they want lunch."

"It depends on how much chicken you have Shorinda because if you don't have enough, I don't want to share."

"In my house, there is always enough. I have a big family who comes over every Sunday. You can be damn sure my kitchen is stocked."

Aliana was excited at the idea of cooking a meal for Hunter. She needed to get a hold of herself. Shorinda winked at her. Dammit. Was she that obvious?

"There's the fixins' for green beans, mashed potatoes, and cornbread. Knock yourself out. I'm going to find something on Netflix. Want to join me, Hunter?"

"I think I'm going to annoy Aliana in the kitchen. I know how to peel potatoes."

Aliana's tummy did a flip. "First, I'm going to go check on *Maminka*."

She went down the hall and found her grandmother in a rocker beside the rented hospital bed. Her mother was smiling.

"Who are you?" she asked Aliana in Czech.

"I'm Aliana, your daughter."

She turned and looked at her mother to validate this information. Obviously, she was in one of her regressed states.

"Yes, Láska, Aliana is your daughter."

"She's so old," her mother whispered.

"Do you want me to brush your hair?" she asked her mother.

"Can you braid it?"

Aliana nodded, then went to work. Her grandmother continued to hum. When Danica fell asleep, both women sighed with relief.

"Babička, I'm making lunch. Why don't you go and take a nap before the food is ready?"

"That might be a good idea."

Aliana looked at the two women who were her world. They both looked so frail. Her heart broke just a little. She went down the hall and asked Shorinda where her grandmother could lie down.

"Let me show you to the guest room."

"This is lovely," her grandmother smiled when Shorinda opened the door to the bright and pretty guest room.

"I'll wake you when lunch is ready."

When they shut the door, Shorinda turned to Aliana. "You know, it might not be a bad idea to have both of them stay with me."

"Great minds think alike," Aliana said.

* * *

"Looks like a pretty boy," Zed said as he watched the big blonde get out of his Audi.

"Takes one to know one," Dalton said with a grin.

Hunter gave his mentor an amused look. He hadn't told him Aiden's name for a reason. He wanted Zed to stick his foot in his mouth. Aiden O'Malley had a bit of a reputation amongst the SEALs, which is why Hunter had only said he was calling in a friend. They were all outside of Shorinda's house on the outskirts of Glendale. Inside were Aliana and her family.

"Nice car," Zed said.

"Thanks," Aiden said, looking Zed up and down. "And you are?"

"I was just about to ask the same question," Zed said looking Aiden over.

Hunter gave a tired smile. The last few days had sucked balls except for his moments with Alia, he'd needed this little break, and the ladies brigade. That had been a fucking riot.

"Chief Petty Officer, Aiden O'Malley, Second in Command of Black Dawn, and you?" Aiden drawled.

"Well, shit. Seems to me Hunter might not have been as forthcoming as he could have been when he said a friend was coming to help out." Zed held out his hand and Aiden slowly shook it. "My name is Dante Zaragoza. I'm with Night Storm out of Virginia."

"I know you. You're Zed."

Well, now that the fun was over, Hunter stepped in.

"Aiden, glad you could make it. We seem to have a bit of a gang problem."

Aiden's blue eyes turned navy. Hunter remembered a drunken night where Aiden had told him a bit about the gang he had dealt with in Chicago.

"What do you need?"

"This is off the books," Hunter said.

"And I repeat myself, what do you need?" Aiden growled.

"I have an old friend who is a target of a major player up here, they're called *Los Demonios*."

"Aliana?" Aiden asked.

Fuck! Just how often had he talked about her?

Dalton clapped him on the shoulder. "You might have mentioned her a time or two over the years."

"Where is she?" Aiden asked.

"She's inside with her sick mother and her grandmother," Hunter answered.

"They need to stay contained. Is this place safe?" Aiden asked.

"Yeah, but it's too small," Hunter answered. "Aliana is going to a hotel. Dalton has one picked out. We're taking her there in the back of an Enterprise van and parking it underground. She'll take the elevators up to her floor, she'll only be on the lobby floor for a minute."

"Sounds good."

"How are we going to work this?" Aiden asked.

"After we get Aliana safely stowed away, we split up. We have some errands to run. I'm going to check in with an old friend of mine and see if he can give me any information on a lowlife named Mateo," Hunter explained. "You and Zed are going to track down this asshole's girlfriend, and Dalton will check out a guy named Rafael."

Everyone nodded.

* * *

Hunter was pissed. LL was thirty-six hours past his allotted time to get him information on Mateo, and he fucking wanted the bastard under his boot. He headed over to the auto body shop in the heart of *Las Nuevas Espadas* territory. It took him a whole thirty seconds to unlock the padlock on the gate. Seriously, they needed to get something that couldn't be undone with a soda can.

"Tex, all you had to do was knock," Martin said as Hunter pushed his bike up to the car bay door.

"Wasn't in the mood."

"And here I thought we were friends since I took the heat for you and got the little broodmare to the hospital."

Hunter shoved his bike into the big man, so the front tire hit him right in the crotch, pinning him to the wall of the building. Martin didn't make a sound. If he wasn't so pissed, Hunter might have admired it.

"Care to repeat that Tex?"

"I didn't know she was important to you," Martin wheezed.

"Let him go, Hunter," LL said softly. Hunter looked up and saw LL staring at him.

"Thought I was going to get some information LL."

A kid who looked like LL came running down the stairs holding a gun. LL looked over his shoulder. "Put that thing away, Lorenzo."

"He's got Martin. Who is he?"

"He's a friend," his father said. "Now put that away. Hunter, pull back the bike. Jesus, I'm surrounded by hotheads."

Hunter backed up the bike, and Martin fell to the ground.

"Come on upstairs," LL motioned to Hunter. "Lorenzo, help Martin."

"What should I do?"

"Take him to the hospital, for God's sake, what the hell do you think you should do?" LL shook his head and motioned Hunter to follow him up to his office.

"Do you have the information I want?" Hunter asked.

"No, I have the information you need," LL responded. "Sit."

"I'll stand." Hunter stood next to the door.

"Suit yourself. Want a drink?" LL asked as he poured himself a scotch.

"Cut the crap and tell me what you think I need to hear."

"San Marcos has a hard-on for Aliana."

"Great, thanks for pointing out the obvious, I think I'll leave now." Hunter turned to open the door.

"Hold up. It's not because he thinks she's extracting his whores. It's because of how she's turned his son against him. Hell, he knows his kid did it. He's just telling his men it's her."

Hunter turned back to stare directly at LL. "How do you know this?"

"I have someone on the inside."

"I thought you said he wasn't telling his men."

"Who said my person is a man?" LL grinned. "Look, he knows exactly what his kid is doing, and he's proud as hell. Thinks he's showing guts and initiative, he's just putting his efforts in the wrong direction."

Hunter turned back to look at LL. "What does he want with Aliana?"

"He's told his men to pick her up because he wants to know where the bitches are hiding, but that's not it at all. He intends to use her as a hostage to keep Nicolas in line."

"That's crazy. How long does he intend to keep her? Twenty fucking years?"

"His thinking is as soon as Nicolas starts seeing how good life can be side-by-side with his old man, he'll change his tune, then he can off your girl. The final blow will be to have Nicolas off Aliana. He has big plans for his boy, and she's fucked them up."

"The man is insane. Has he met his son?"

"Sure he has," LL laughed. "He thinks rainbows shoot out of his ass. He wants him to rule beside him."

"If he thinks so goddamn highly of him, why'd he throw him away, why didn't he raise him, himself?"

"Nicolas' mom died in childbirth. San Marcos had her sister raise the kid. Hell, he was fifteen when the kid was born."

That meant that Ana Garcia was Nicolas' aunt and Mateo was his cousin. Okay, Hunter could buy this.

"I still don't get why San Marcos doesn't just tell Nicolas to stop his shit. Why get Aliana involved?"

"As much as San Marcos thinks his son is God's gift, he knows his son worships your Aliana. He knows that the only way to get Nicolas to come to heel is to use the bitch as leverage."

"LL, don't call her a bitch again, are we clear?" Hunter flavored his tone with ice.

LL held up his hands. "No disrespect."

"So why did he try to kill her if he had this grand plan to use her as leverage?"

"You're still not getting it, are you?" LL asked. "That wasn't San Marcos that was that dumb shit Mateo. That boy is many bricks shy of a full load."

"He's worse than that, LL. He's a pedophile. He was raping his sister. I don't know how old she was when it started. He needs to be taken off the board."

"Are you fucking kidding me?" LL slammed down his drink on his desk.

"Where the fuck can I find San Marcos?"

"Shit, Hunter, if I knew that, I would have taken him out years ago. I have your information on Mateo though. He lives with his girlfriend, and I know where she lives."

"I've already got that information."

"Well, shit."

Lorenzo and Martin were gone when he got outside. He checked in with Aiden and Zed. They had Mateo's girlfriend's place staked out. Dalton said he'd stashed Aliana and now had something cooking. He'd get back to him. So, Hunter had some time on his hands. He knew exactly how he planned to spend it.

CHAPTER TWELVE

When he got to the underground garage, he texted Aliana and got no response. He called her, still nothing. He took the stairs up to her floor three at a time. When he got to her door, he started out with a soft knock. Nothing. Then he pounded.

He heard a muffled 'Hunter' before the door was opened, which at least told him she'd used the peephole. She stood there in a towel, her blonde hair billowing around her.

"What's wrong?" she cried.

"You didn't answer your phone," he pushed her inside with his body, then closed the door. Holy hell, she was almost naked. Scratch that, she was naked underneath that towel. Granted, it was a big hotel towel, but it was a towel.

"I was blow drying my hair. It's loud, and it takes forever. You didn't tell me what's wrong."

"Nothing."

"Let me get dressed."

Not on my account. But he didn't say it out loud.

She hadn't packed clothes when she'd left her grandmother's house, so Shorinda had given her some to borrow. He was interested to see what the short and curvy nurse had to offer that would fit.

Aliana's hand reached out of the bathroom. "Hunter can you pass in the hotel robe. I think I saw in the closet."

"Why?"

"These don't fit. They're too tight."

"Huh? That doesn't make sense." But he had an idea of what was going on, and he wanted to see.

"She told me she kept her skinny clothes. But because she's shorter, she thought the yoga outfits might work. They don't."

Yep. Spandex.

"It's just me," he coaxed.

"Hunter, give me the robe," her tone brooked no argument. God, the Vice Principal voice made him hot. He handed her the robe.

She came out rocking the robe like a queen.

"I really wanted to see the yoga outfit."

"It was lime green, it would have clashed with the last of the bruises," she said haughtily. "So, tell me what's going on."

He looked around the room. Dalton had done well, it was a mini-suite with a couch and a coffee table. He saw she'd already taken a nap on the king-sized bed.

"Let's sit down." He went over and grabbed a Snickers bar, a bag of chocolate chip cookies, and a bottle of water off the refreshment table.

"Hunter, those cost a mint. There's a vending machine down the hall."

"I'll worry about it some other time. Anyway, Aiden's here now. He can pay for the hotel."

"I'm paying for my own hotel, and of course, you can have whatever you want. I'm sorry I said anything." God, she was cute.

"I was teasing about Aiden. I'm paying for your hotel." But he knew his friend, he'd be paying. Somehow, it'd magically happen. He was fucking annoying about shit like that.

"I'm not going to argue with you, just tell me what's going on. This is my problem, I want to know about the investigation."

God, she had like some sort of sexy kitten growl going on. He shifted on the couch so he could adjust his jeans. The last thing she needed is to see how aroused he was when she was alone in a hotel room with him wearing nothing but a robe.

"You met Aiden."

"Right before you stuffed me in the back of a van. He seemed nice," she rolled her eyes.

"He and Zed are staking out Mateo's girlfriend's apartment. Dalton has a lead on Rafael, and I went and visited LL, who finally had some decent information to offer."

"He was Rita's boyfriend, right? You used to talk about him occasionally."

"He's Rita's husband now. They have four daughters and a son," Hunter scowled.

"What?"

"What is with all these assholes thinking it's cool to get their kids into the gang life. I would think they would want what's good for them. Do you know what happened to most of the kid's I hung out with? Dead, prison, and crippled." He stood up and raked his hands through his hair. He thought specifically of Felix. Hell, he had friends he'd served with who had ended up losing limbs or in wheelchairs, but they had done something honorable. Not sold drugs.

He turned around and Aliana was in front of him.

"Tell me."

"LL has his kid, Lorenzo, running prostitutes, he's so proud of him. What the fuck, Alia? How could my friend's thinking be so fucked up?"

"I don't know." She put her hands on his chest.

"Cariña, I need you to sit back down."

"Why?"

"It gets worse."

"Is this about Nicolas? I'd prefer to take my news standing."

"San Marcos is just as determined or maybe even more determined than LL that Nicolas is going to take over *Los Demonios*."

Aliana's eyes sparkled, and her laughter filled the room. "Yeah, that's not going to happen. That boy is bound and determined to take down his father's organization. I love him."

"No, he has a plan."

"Yeah, I know he does. We have to stop him. We have to get him out of town. We need to convince him to have the church find him a place in the Midwest to hide. He's done."

"San Marcos knows what he's doing. He's actually pretty proud of his boy. Thinks it shows initiative and leadership. Just the kind of qualities he needs to one day hand over *Los Demonios*."

"You know, Mark didn't strike me as crazy when I met him. Kind of scary, but not nuts. I guess my radar was off."

Hunter grabbed her left hand in his and then stroked back her wild blonde hair so he could cup her warm cheek. "He has a plan, *mi Cielieto*, he holds you hostage and forces Nicolas to cooperate."

She looked at him, confused. "I don't get it, why did he try to kill me?"

"He didn't, Mateo did. Mateo isn't Nicolas' brother, he's his cousin. San Marcos didn't want him to do that, Mateo was acting on his own. We need to find San Marcos, and he's hiding deep. LL is looking for him. We need to find one of his lieutenants who can lead him to us, and since we already have a couple of leads on Mateo, we're going to pull that string."

Aliana had clutched his jacket as he told her what he'd heard. He wanted more. He shrugged out of his coat and took off his holster. She stared at his gun as he set it down on the side table next to the couch.

"Hunter," she said softly, "I'm really kind of liking that out-of-state option."

He pulled her into his arms. "I know, *mi Amor*. This is going to be over in just a couple of more days. You'll go back to being a kick-ass Vice Principal, and this will all be in the past. Well, everything but us."

She pushed against his chest so she could look into his eyes. Now he saw fear in her eyes for another reason, but behind that, he saw hope. He could work with hope.

Her eyes darted around the room, then she looked down at her robe and she looked back up at him. "Hunter, I, uhm."

"Easy, Alia, there isn't a chance in hell I want to make love with you five minutes after I tell you some madman is out to kidnap you."

"Oh," she started to bite her lip, and stopped herself, and licked it instead.

"Well, damn woman, if you tempt me like that, I take it back." He couldn't hide the desire from his voice.

She started to say something and then stopped.

"What?"

She looked down at his chest, then up at him through her lashes. "Do you think we could kiss again?"

God save him. "Yes, we could definitely kiss again." He pictured kissing her in that rumpled bed and thought better of it. He led her around the coffee table and pulled her into his arms. She jerked and pulled the robe tight around her legs.

"Easy, everything's fine. It's just a kiss, *mi Cielieto*, nothing more."

Her eyes cut away from his.

"Alia, it's okay if you've changed your mind." He leaned back and eased her against his chest. "Just holding you is the stuff of dreams."

She looked back at him. "I feel special when you hold me. I always have."

He should have come back years ago. But then again, had he been ready? Would she have been? He eyed her critically—the bruising had faded more, her lips didn't look swollen, just tempting—but he had to be sure.

"Does your head hurt?"

"Hunter, kiss me," her warm breath wafted over him as she touched her lips to his.

Her soft heat was incredible, and he wondered how such a delicate touch could be so powerful. He let her lead, but when her tongue came out to trace the seam of his lips, she hesitated and stopped. His eyes drifted open and collided with her panicked blue ones. He cupped her cheeks and drew her back.

"What is it, *mi Amor*?"

"You're not doing anything. What am I doing wrong?" Her voice was tremulous, and he could see she was about to cry.

"Oh, Alia, you're doing everything right. You were perfect. I was wrapped up in your kiss. I thought you wanted to lead."

"I don't want to lead," she said as her fingers bit into his chest. "I want you to. I like it when you do. It's just, you were taking too long."

Oh, he could lead, all right. He sifted his fingers through her hair, enjoying her look of pleasure. He cupped the back of her neck, his other hand dipping down beneath her robe just a bit, bringing her inexorably closer. He slanted her head so it was just right when their lips met.

He took possession of the tender treasure, molding her lips to his. She flowered open, and he savored the warm, wet heat, loving how she sought her pleasure. Aliana slid her tongue against his, and he kneaded the taut muscles in the back of her neck, his other hand sliding further down her spine, allowing himself this small taste of her skin.

She released her desperate grip on the front of his t-shirt and speared one hand into his hair, raking her nails against his scalp. He groaned his rapture, arching into the caress. Then his world stilled when he felt her other hand slip under the hem of his shirt and steal its way up his stomach, setting fire to every nerve in his body.

Hunter slowly shifted their positions so she was lying on the sofa. He hated that he had to pull his hand away from the silken skin of her back, but tracing her collarbone was no hardship. He was careful to make sure his body didn't press against hers. He didn't want to overwhelm her, but it was difficult because *Cielieto* had both arms wrapped around him and was pulling him ever downward.

He released her mouth and pressed her face into the crook of his neck, trying to gain a modicum of control, but it was one of the hardest things he'd ever had to do, especially as her untried body swayed upwards toward him.

"Hunter?"

"I'm here, *mi Amor*, I have you."

"That's my favorite," she sighed. Her foot was rubbing against his calf. He knew what that meant. If he looked down, her knee would be next to his thigh, her legs parted. He needed to think of something else. Anything else.

"What's your favorite?"

"I love it when you call me my love," she breathed the words into his ears, and it went straight to his cock. He was struggling to keep his body poised those few inches above hers, not touching. Not lying on, not pressing into…

Then she licked the side of his neck.

"Alia, you don't know what you're doing."

"I know we won't go too far."

He swept his hand down, determined to do the right thing. He grabbed the terry cloth of the robe so he could wrap it back around her. But by God, he would at least look before he covered her up. A shapely leg that went forever, silky white skin he wanted to explore, touch and taste. When he touched her thigh, she jolted as if lightning had struck her body. Hunter felt the change in the texture of the skin underneath his fingertips. Silk turned ragged as he found line after line after line of scar tissue.

"No," Alia sounded agonized, but she didn't move. No other word escaped her lips. He looked up into her blue eyes wide with fear. What was she scared of? He eased off the couch and knelt beside it, cupping her face.

"It's going to be all right." Then awareness exploded through his brain, and his heart ached. He knew reassuring her was the most important thing. "Alia, *Cariña*, it doesn't matter."

Fuck, that was the wrong thing to say because it sure as fuck did matter. His woman had been hurting so desperately that somehow cutting herself was the only way she could find solace. Goddamn right, it mattered.

Aliana must have seen it on his face because she whimpered and pressed herself back against the couch, tears welling in her eyes.

"No, Baby, no. You've misunderstood. I'm not mad, at least not at you. I just ache at the thought you were hurting so badly, you had to do this to yourself." He rested his palm on the five inch by six-inch patch of scarred flesh on her right thigh. He could tell the scars were years old, but still, he wanted to somehow warm the spot. Heal it. Make it feel better.

"It's ugly."

"No, it's not," he defended immediately.

She covered his hand with her own. "Yes, it is, I've looked at it for years. It's horrible," her voice sounded like her throat was filled with broken glass.

He looked down again, getting a flash of lace black panties underneath the robe. At any other time that would have been delightful, but not now. He moved his hand and really looked at the lacerated flesh. His brain didn't register scars, it just didn't, every single precise cut indicated a story, a wound on her soul. Was she healed? Could he help?

He bent his head and feathered kiss after kiss on her scarred skin, all the while she stroked his hair and whispered his name. Finally, he looked up.

"Can you tell me? Was this going on while I was living here?"

She shook her head, blonde hair flying everywhere.

"When?"

"My senior year."

"Can you tell me?"

She closed her eyes and sighed, then opened them again. She looked at him, really looked at him. "You understand, don't you? How come?"

"A friend of mine's younger brother did it. The kid had words cut into the back of his hands when he showed up at graduation, so Ollie explained it."

"Oh. Is he okay now?"

"I don't know. Ollie was discharged, and we didn't keep in touch. Can you tell me what started it?" He needed to know. Had to know. "Was it because I stopped writing letters?"

She leaned forward, "Oh Hunter, God no. This had nothing to do with you. This was me. Something went wrong. I broke. Junior year things escalated at school," she swallowed and looked away.

"What happened?"

"It doesn't matter," she said, tugging her robe close around herself.

"It does."

She swung around to look at him, her eyes furious.

"No, it doesn't. It was the same kind of stuff as always, they were just older, and the pranks were more sophisticated, but my defenses weren't any better," she said bitterly. "Hunter, I had problems. I had no real coping skills, and I didn't learn them until I got to college and met Dr. Taylor. She was incredible. She didn't save me, she helped me to save myself. But it was a long hard road, and it still takes vigilance. Even now."

"What do you mean, *Cariña*?" he kept his voice soft.

"It was like my drug, for me it alleviated stress and pain. When I feel that now, I flash to that. Sometimes the urge is so strong, it's incredible." Her hands clenched in the material of her robe until her knuckles turned white. "But I guess the good news is, I've fought it." She gave him a tentative smile. "You help me to fight."

He arched a brow in question.

She lifted her right hand and pulled a long chain out from under her robe. Hunter saw the gold medallion swinging in her grasp.

"This Hunter. It's helped me for years. I've kept it close to me ever since you gave it to me."

His heart stuttered.

"So, in the end? Except for the last couple of days, my life's had a happy ending. I beat the bitches." Then she leaned forward, and he got a glimpse of the tops of her breasts, he looked away. "Do you want to know something?" she asked in a whisper.

"Always."

"I've checked up on them."

"Who?"

"Heather, Lupita and Theresa," she grinned. "Wanna know a little about their lives?"

Hunter loved the sparkle in her eye. "Abso-fucking-lutely."

"Lupita got caught stealing from the till at McDonald's. It was the third time. She's currently in county lockup."

"I don't know what happened to Theresa, but the best is Heather."

"Lay it on me."

"Remember how she always said she was going to make it big in Hollywood?"

Hunter nodded.

"Well, she did end up on TV."

"Okay," Hunter said slowly.

"Yep," Aliana grinned. "She was working at one of the brothels in Vegas and on a cable reality show. Her specialty was groups, but then her teeth started coming loose. It turned out she was doing meth, so she ended up losing her job."

"Couldn't happen to a nicer gal."

"You don't think I'm horrible that I laughed my ass off, and re-watched the episode where her tooth fell out? I drank champagne."

"Hell no. Do you have it saved on your DVR? Because I want to watch it too," Hunter smiled broadly.

"Thanks, Hunter."

"For what?"

"Just for being you. For being part of my past, for not judging me, for being here for me now."

"You forgot the most important thing."

"What?" she asked.

"You forgot to mention I'm going to be part of your future. Now, let's get some clothes on you and order some pizza. If I can't have one appetite fed, then we're feeding my other one."

She let out a peal of laughter.

God, he was in love with Aliana Mila Novak.

CHAPTER THIRTEEN

After the call from Dalton, Hunter got on his bike and headed toward downtown. On a Saturday night, heading toward downtown L.A., traffic was still a bitch. But Hunter took advantage of the law that let him lane split and dodged in between the cars. He made great time down to the hotel. He pulled up to the valet.

When he got to the front of the line, a white guy looked him up and down. "I'm sorry Sir, we don't park motorcycles here at the Valet. Are you a guest?"

"I'm meeting a friend."

"You'll need to park in our underground garage. Just follow the curve down to the right." The young man pointed him in the correct direction. Hunter drove his bike slowly, surveying all the valet attendants as he went. It wasn't until he was almost to the garage that he saw a young Hispanic man running up from the garage stairs. He'd bet his bottom dollar it was Rafael.

Hunter took the ticket to get into the garage, parked on the bottom floor near the valet section, far enough away so his bike wouldn't be dinged by any other cars, and took the stairs two at a time up to the lobby. Dalton was relaxing on one of the couches talking to a striking older woman. He had managed to fit into the exclusive environment, even in jeans, t-shirt, and leather jacket. Dalton spotted Hunter immediately and excused himself and came over to him.

"Did you see our guy?" he asked.

"Think so. Cross tattoo showing a little on his right hand?" Hunter asked.

"That'd be him."

"How d'you find him?"

"Scoped out the apartment building Nicolas mentioned. Figured he'd be working on a Saturday night. Looked for any kid wearing pants other than jeans. He made it easy because he was carrying his valet jacket on a hanger. He took the train. I followed him."

Hunter grinned. That was Dalton, always thinking. "How should we play it?"

"I say question him now. He'll be more apt to talk if he needs to get rid of us to save his job."

Not a bad plan.

They took the stairs down to the level where the valeted cars were parked. Hunter stepped out first. There were plenty of pillars between the door and the entrance ramp where he could hide. "Wanna stay here?" he asked Dalton.

"Yep."

"I'll head over there," he pointed to a spot close to the down ramp.

The first car that pulled in was driven by the same valet who had told him where to park. The young man eased the BMW into a space close to the stairs.

"Shit. Fuck. Piss." Hunter swore under his breath, then he texted Dalton.

Incoming.

When the valet opened the door to the stairs thirty seconds later, there was no sign of Dalton. A white Mercedes AMG came down the ramp rounding the corner at a fast clip. Hunter saw only dark hair driving by, and he watched it go to the far wall. He saw a door to what he assumed was the maintenance closet open. He crouched low and moved fast, keeping in the shadows.

"They're staying two nights. They left their house keys on the ring. Their address is listed on some mail in the glovebox. Quick, Mateo, take an imprint of the keys," Rafael said in Spanish to a young Hispanic man.

Another car pulled in, the headlights caught Hunter.

"Fuck," Mateo said in Spanish. He pulled out a gun and fired at Hunter, then ripped Rafael out of the Mercedes and threw him to the ground. He got into the high-performance sports car and squealed backward behind the Escalade that had just pulled into the garage, then did a one-eighty. Hunter couldn't get off a shot without hitting the big black vehicle. He ran around it, but by that time the Mercedes was going up the ramp.

Dalton ran out of the stairwell, his gun drawn.

"White Mercedes AMG," Hunter yelled. "It's Mateo. Rafael's on the ground," he waved backward. He was on his motorcycle in a heartbeat. By the time Hunter got to the top of the parking structure, he saw the car had ripped through the parking garage's gate and had to swerve to avoid the broken wood on the ground. He saw the taillights of the white car going down Figueroa Street.

A game or a concert must have let out of the Staples Center, making traffic bad, really bad. Hunter weaved around cars, trying to catch up to the supercharged Mercedes. Fuck, did it have to be the AMG edition? Mateo took a turn onto Flower street, hitting a homeless man's shopping cart, sending the man sprawling, his contents going everywhere. Hunter skidded sideways, barely missing the exploding plastic bags containing the man's life.

The growl of his bike was loud without his helmet. He revved up his throttle and sped faster, then Mateo merged onto the 110 Freeway, and the race was really on. His bike got up to speeds he'd never seen before. Where was the California Highway Patrol when you needed them?

Mateo weaved in and out of traffic until finally, he couldn't. Three lanes were blocked, two tractor trailers and one Prius all going the same speed. Hunter fell far back, hoping Mateo would think he'd lost him and stop the crazy-assed driving, and no lives would be lost on the freeway. He kept an eye on him, but the fucker darted forward when there was an opening and the game was on again.

Up ahead, he saw blue and red lights flashing as the highway patrol raced to catch up with the performance car. Again, Hunter fell back, watching.

Mateo must have realized he was at the end of the line because he sped up even more. Hunter could see the accident happening in his mind's eye before it did. Mateo headed for the exit, but he hadn't read the exit closure signs. He crashed through the orange signs straight into the cement barriers, and flipped the stolen car, disappearing over the side of the exit ramp. Hunter saw flames shoot up. The highway patrol skidded to a stop while Hunter kept driving down the freeway toward the next exit.

When Hunter was finally able to pull over to a stop on a side street, he patted the side of his bike. Damn, she had performed well. He fished his phone out of the deep jacket pocket and called Dalton.

"Where the fuck are you?"

"Still trying to figure that out. Got Rafael?" Adrenaline was pumped wildly through his veins. He quickly calculated how much information Rafael could give them about the threat against Aliana, hopefully, it hadn't died with Mateo.

"I've got him and your helmet. He and I are having a nice little chat in the back of the 7-11 on Hope Street. You might want to join us."

"On it."

* * *

"Did you call Zed and Aiden?" Hunter asked as he dismounted the bike and ambled towards the two men, never taking his eyes off the cowering former valet.

"Yep. They said if we needed any help with clean up to call them."

"Clean up?" Rafael squeaked.

"Was I talking to you?" Dalton asked as he cuffed him on the side of the head. "You talk when I tell you to talk." Rafael whimpered.

"Careful Dalton, according to Aliana and Nicolas this guy might be on the side of the angels."

"Yeah, sure he is, stealing cars, breaking into people's homes. He's a regular Mother Teresa. The way I heard it, he was there when Aliana was attacked, and he planted a bomb in her home. That makes him more than an asshole, that makes him an attempted murderer. This is not going to go down well."

"You don't understand, I was trying to save her life." Hunter could see the whites of Rafael's eyes, and by the sound of his voice, you'd never think he'd hit puberty.

"Rafe, you don't need to worry about a police charge," Hunter soothed. He took three steps forward, so he was towering over him. "Aliana is my woman. Do you think I'm going to let you see the inside of a cell?"

"You've got to believe me. She was my teacher in school. She was cool. I really liked her. I wouldn't do anything to hurt her."

"There is only one way for this to come down so you don't end up like Mateo, and that's if you provide the right information," Hunter whispered softly.

"What happened to Mateo?"

"Yeah, what? Inquiring minds want to know," Dalton chimed in.

"He's dead, burned to death." Rafael flinched and started to tremble. "It's a bad way to go Rafael. Do you want to burn to death?" The kid opened his mouth, but no words came out. "Answer me," Hunter barked.

"No," he squeaked.

"Where is San Marcos? I want an address."

"He'll kill me."

"Hold on Hunter," Dalton laughed. "The 7-11 sells lighters." He turned to leave.

"No! Don't," Rafael pleaded. "You'll never beat San Marcos, and he'll find out I'm the one who gave you the information. He won't just kill me, he'll kill my dad."

"So leave town," Dalton said over his shoulder. Hunter knew his teammate would be back soon with anything fire related the convenience store had to offer. It wouldn't be necessary, Rafael would talk before then.

"Tell me. You know he's after Aliana, you don't want him to get his hands on her."

"Man, it's inevitable. He knows everything. He knows where her mom is, her grandma even that damn shrink with the killer shoes."

Hunter froze. Goddammit, they hadn't been watching Lottie. Hunter picked the kid up by the front of his sky blue valet jacket.

"Tell me where he lives. I need an address, Rafael, or so help me God, I really will set you on fire."

"I don't know where he lives, but he does all his business out of a tattoo parlor on El Fenix and Seabreeze. He keeps like office hours."

Hunter moved his wrist and saw that it was a little past eleven p.m. "Will he be there now?"

"Guaranteed."

He pulled out his phone, called Zed, and told him to get to Lottie's place.

Hunter looked across the street at the long-term parking lot. It would work. He called Dalton.

"Get duct tape."

* * *

Aliana looked down at her cell phone and smiled. She had so much to share with her friend, and the snoopy, shrinky part of Lottie would be all agog at the information.

"It's about time you called me back," Aliana smiled.

"Hi, Ms. Novak, it's Mark. Were you expecting your friend Carlotta?" he asked in Spanish.

Aliana had to bring up her other hand and use both of them to keep the phone next to her ear, otherwise, she would have dropped it. She took a calming breath.

"Hello, Mark, may I please speak with my friend?" she asked pleasantly.

"So polite, I like that about you. You've taught my son so many good qualities. I appreciate that. You've also taught him some undesirable ones as well. We talked about that Ms. Novak, or can I call you Aliana?"

"Ms. Novak is fine."

"Aliana, I told you to stay away from my son. I told you not to fill his head with ideas that wouldn't help him in this world, but what did you do? You turned him into a goddamned revolutionary."

"Let me talk to Lottie."

"No. I'm not going to give you that courtesy because you didn't give me the courtesy of doing what I asked."

"Then what is the point of this call?" she asked politely.

She just had to keep it together for just a moment, then she would call Hunter. Hunter would know what to do.

"I want us to have a little visit."

She opened her mouth to tell him she knew about his plans for her, but then shut it. Was she supposed to know? Was there an informant involved?

"I don't trust you. Mateo threatened my mother. He said he would cut her up into pieces. I was almost killed when my townhome was blown up. Nope. I think I'll pass on your little invite."

She might be many things, but she refused to be in the too stupid to live camp.

"If you don't meet with me, I'll kill your friend."

"Let me talk to her."

There was silence. Then she heard a muffled roar and the unmistakable sound of someone being slapped.

"Bitch," Mark roared.

"Aliana, is that you?" Lottie asked, panting.

"Why did he slap you?" Aliana cried.

"Don't do anything he says," Lottie was crying so hard, she could barely understand her.

She heard a muffled scream. "There you talked to Lottie. As you can see, she's not making friends. It will be my pleasure to kill her if you don't trade places with her."

"Cut the crap, Mark. You'll just kill us both," Aliana said derisively.

Fuck. Her brain started to work. Hell, if she didn't start sounding like she was giving in, then Lottie would be killed for sure. Way to outsmart the situation.

"Fine. I'll kill her and find another way to get you. I'm sorry to have—"

"No, no, no. Tell me what to do. Don't hurt her."

"Tell me where you are," he demanded.

"I'm being guarded," she lied. "I don't want there to be a bloodbath with people I care about. Let me sneak away. Tell me where I need to meet you, and I'll go there." She walked over to the hotel desk and wrote down the address he provided.

"A car will be waiting for you. You better come alone."

"I will. I promise."

He hung up and she called Hunter and got his voicemail.

* * *

Lottie's house was ten minutes from the school, right in the heart of *Los Demonios* territory. Aiden and Zed were already inside when Hunter and Dalton both pulled up on his motorcycle. They both hightailed it inside. Hunter stopped short when he saw the look on Zed's face.

"What happened?"

"There was quite a struggle in the bedroom. Lottie's gone. Based on his ID, Ernie Robinson is dead."

"Fuck." Hunter had really liked the guy. "Any idea how long ago this happened?"

"We're in luck. There was a kitschy alarm clock broken in her bedroom. Happened at ten forty-five," Aiden said.

Dalton, Zed, and Hunter all stared at Aiden.

"What?"

"Just looking at the man who correctly used kitschy in a sentence is all." Aiden flipped Dalton the bird. At least the tension was eased, and they could think again.

"Fuck!" Hunter jammed his hand into his jacket pocket. "San Marcos is going to go straight to Aliana to make a trade." When he pulled out his phone, he saw four voicemails and seven missed calls, all from his Alia. The last one was seven minutes ago. Please God, say he wasn't too late. He dialed and waited. He got her voicemail.

"Aliana, don't go. Wherever he's having you meet him, don't do it. We know where to find him. We'll get Lottie. Don't go, I'm begging you."

He motioned for Dalton to fill in Zed and Aiden on what they'd found out from Rafael. He turned on the locator app he'd installed on Aliana's phone the first night. Goddammit, she wasn't in the hotel where he'd left her. What was she doing near Bertrum High School? His phone rang. It was her.

"Aliana, what's going on?"

"You didn't listen to my voicemails, did you?"

"I just saw them. Why are you near the high school? Is that where the meet is going down with San Marcos?"

"I never made it to him. I was ambushed." She didn't sound hurt.

"What the fuck do you mean you were ambushed. Alia, are you all right?" All three men were now giving him intent looks.

"Yes, I'm fine. But I'm worried as hell about Lottie. Mark has her, and I didn't make the meeting, I was—"

"Goddammit, Aliana, tell me where the fuck you are," Hunter roared.

"Come to the front of the high school. I'm in a black suburban. I'm with Nicolas and two of his friends."

He'd started out the door as soon as she started to tell him where she was. He was on his bike by the time she said she was with Nicolas. If there was a God, he would have made it there by the time she had finished speaking, but instead, it required seven extra minutes. He pulled out his gun and aimed it at the driver.

"Come out with your hands up."

"Hunter, these are friends," Aliana yelled as she opened up the left rear door.

"Aliana, go sit on the curb."

Aiden, Zed, and Dalton were beside him. The Audi was fast. They all had their guns drawn. Two Hispanic boys who probably hadn't started shaving got out of the SUV with their hands up as well as a grinning Nicolas. Hunter didn't know whether to hug him or beat the shit out of him. What the fuck was going on?

"Can I get up now?" Aliana was sitting on the cold cement, wearing a turquoise tunic and drawstring pants she'd bought from the hotel gift store. She had her hand up like she was in class, but her expression was hardly that of a student, it was more of a pissed off Vice Principal.

Now that he knew everything was in hand, he rushed over to her and swept her into his arms. He palmed the back of her head and searched her eyes, assuring himself she was okay. Please, say she hadn't been traumatized.

Aliana wound her arms around his neck. "I knew you'd come."

He crushed his lips against hers. He tried to get a modicum of control, but there was none to be had. She opened for him, welcomed him. The hot, sultry, Southern California air curled around them, adding another layer of heat to a kiss that was out of control.

"Hey, we have a mission here. Remember?" Zed yelled out.

"They can't hear us. They're deaf to the world," Dalton laughed.

"Shut it, you two. Just wait til it happens to you," Aiden said.

"Ms. Novak?" Nicolas whispered quietly. Aliana immediately started to pull away.

Hunter tucked her face into the crook of his neck, turning to look at Nicolas.

"Son, can you give us a report?" He watched as the young man's shoulders straightened, and he looked at him and each of his teammates in turn.

"My real dad has Ms. Rodriguez. He's going to use her to hurt you, Ms. Novak."

"Sperm donor," her words muffled as she said them into his shoulder. She pushed away from him and twisted to look at Nicolas. "He's not your father Nicolas. He's nothing more than a sperm donor. A father is someone who nurtures you and takes care of you. This asshole did nothing more than supply some DNA. He's not your dad, Honey."

Hunter watched as the kid brightened. Jesus, here they were in the middle of a kidnapping, potential torture mess, and she's working on lifting up a kid's self-esteem. First, he was going to kill some people, then he was going to figure out what mountains he had to move, but goddammit, he was not going to lose Aliana ever again.

"Hunter," she whispered.

"Yeah?"

"You're kind of squeezing me a little too tightly." Her eyes were dancing.

He kissed the tip of her nose and loosened his hold. He turned to the others.

"Okay, we need a plan."

CHAPTER FOURTEEN

Fuck. Fuck. Fuck. What in the hell was Lorenzo doing at the tattoo parlor? Hunter might have thought he had come prepared, but he was an amateur compared to Dalton and Aiden. That's how he was on the roof across the street with a pair of high powered binoculars which allowed him to see into the second floor window of the tattoo parlor.

It was as if the talk about Heather's life at the brothel were coming to life. There were San Marcos and Lorenzo sitting side-by-side on the couch each getting blowjobs while Lottie was tied up across the room looking like she was in some sort of trance.

Hunter would love to just take the shot and be done with it, but there were at least fifteen gang members downstairs. Nope, they needed to stick to the plan. It rested with Zed. He hadn't been spotted outside Mrs. J's house. He could definitely come in as a player who needed to talk to San Marcos.

It would be a stretch for Aiden or Dalton to pull it off. The one hitch in the plan would be if anyone remembered him from years ago.

Meanwhile, Dalton and Aiden were getting into position. There was a closed beauty salon to the right of the tattoo parlor, and Dalton was going in through the back. Aiden occasionally enjoyed heights, so he was doing some second story work in the accountant's office to the left of the tattoo parlor. Hunter wasn't thrilled being relegated to conductor. But, on the upside, thanks to Aiden, he had a rifle, so he might get to have some fun.

"Can you three hear me?" Hunter whispered into his mic. When he got affirmatives, he explained what he saw going on with San Marcos. "Lorenzo is LL's seventeen-year-old son."

"Is he a traitor to his dad or working undercover?" Aiden asked.

"He's not bright enough for undercover," Hunter sighed. Shit, this was going to kill LL.

"This doesn't impact the plan, does it?" Zed asked.

"Nope," Hunter responded. "Go for it."

He watched as Zed drove Aiden's Audi up the street to the parlor and double parked. He couldn't hear clearly through all the commotion, but he knew people were telling him he couldn't park there. Zed, in his normal friendly manner, said something that had everyone backing away with their hands up and ushering him into the parlor.

When he got into the parlor, it was easier to hear what he was saying.

"My business is with San Marcos," Zed said in Spanish.

"I'm Esteban, tonight you talk to me." Esteban looked like he had served thirty years in Attica and had scared even the warden.

Zed took four steps forward until they were nose-to-nose. "Esteban, you seem like a really nice guy, but I didn't drive all the way from San Diego to talk to the help. I can make this operation a million dollars in a weeks time, but if getting his dick sucked is too important to San Marcos, I'll just take this deal to LL."

Hunter believed him, hook line and sinker. Zed shouldn't be in the Navy, he should be in the movies. Esteban believed him too. He didn't say a word, he just turned around and sauntered through a door that led to the back stairs.

Hunter could see San Marcos was pissed to be interrupted. It wasn't that bad, he had the woman continue with what she was doing the entire time Esteban talked to him. Both Esteban and San Marcos seemed to realize at the same moment they were discussing something they shouldn't in front of Lorenzo because they looked over at him. San Marcos tilted his head toward the kid, and Esteban got the message. Before Hunter had a chance to react, Esteban took out his gun and shot Lorenzo in the head.

The two young women started screaming. It was the perfect diversion.

"Aiden, Dalton, Go."

Esteban dragged the two girls away from the couch by their hair and threw them down onto the floor, close to where

Lottie was tied. San Marcos was up and zipped. Esteban was out the door first, then shots started. In an instant, San Marcos' entire demeanor changed. He looked around the room, saw Lorenzo's body, the two crying women, and Lottie who was totally zoned out. He cocked his head and listened to the shots. He shook his head and pulled out his gun and aimed it at the woman tied to the chair.

Hunter pulled the rifle's trigger and watched San Marco's head explode. Lottie was safe.

"Lottie's upstairs on the second floor. Make sure nobody goes upstairs," Hunter said into the mic. He grabbed his gear and headed off the roof.

When he hit the pavement, he saw two black Escalades pulling up behind the Audi. LL was one of the first ones out of the SUV. He ran into the tattoo parlor as Dalton came out carrying Lottie, Aiden followed him, with Zed in the rear.

"Zed, take the Audi and get Lottie to a hospital. All hell is *really* about to break loose inside. We need to be gone."

Dalton gently placed Lottie into the passenger seat and buckled her in. Yelling, screaming, and automatic gunfire was heard from inside. As soon as the door was closed, Zed sped down the street. Hunter and his teammates hauled ass down one block and over three to Zed's piece of shit rental.

Hunter couldn't get back to Aliana fast enough.

* * *

"*Cariña*, wake up."

Aliana hurt. It took a moment to realize she had been sleeping in a chair beside her best friend's hospital bed. She looked up and there was Hunter. He looked ragged.

"Are you okay?" she asked in a whisper.

"Can you come with me?" He held out his hand, helped her up, and took her to the corner of the room, away from Lottie.

"What's going on?"

"Nicolas' family is all sorts of fucked up at the moment, and Ana Garcia is in a lot of pain. I was hoping you could work some of your magic."

"What's going on?"

"As much of a monster as he was, Mateo was still her son, and he died last night. There are complications with Darla's pregnancy, so she has to stay in the hospital longer, and Nicolas is peppering her with questions about his real mom, and she seems to be at her breaking point."

Aliana listened to what he said, but that didn't explain why he looked as though he'd gone through the ringer.

"*Mi Amor*, I asked you if you were okay," she repeated quietly.

"Dex warned me about getting a smart one, said if I did, I'd never get away with shit."

He was scaring her. She grabbed his big hand in hers and held it against her chest.

"Just tell me what's wrong."

"I've been called away on a mission. We go wheels up

tonight. I just found out. I've got to leave in the next twenty minutes." He looked like he was in pain. There were lines of stress on his forehead and his dimples were nowhere to be found.

"When are you going to be back?"

"I don't know, Alia. We're going in blind. I should be able to call in a week. Maybe send an email." His voice trailed off. What wasn't he saying?

"Hunter, what does going in blind mean?"

"It means I won't know where we're headed until we get on the plane. Then we'll find out the location and mission parameters. That means it's hot. Sometimes those are fast and to the point, but sometimes they can be protracted."

"Hunter, what's the longest mission you've ever been on?"

"Five months." He put his arm around her waist and bent closer so they could see each other's eyes better in the dim light of the hospital room. "But Alia, that was only one time. They're mostly two to three weeks, but if I'm laying my cards on the table, there was another one that lasted three months. And I know that Zed's team had one that lasted almost a year."

That was her Hunter, honest to a fault.

"Honey, it's okay. This is your job. You serve our country. I respect that."

"Yeah, but can you live with it?"

"We're going to find out, now aren't we?" She smiled the best she could. "Now that we've wasted five minutes, could I please get my goodbye kiss?"

Despite her teasing, he was still concerned. It was time to

take matters into her own hands. She grabbed his ears and pulled his head down to hers. He broke out into a grin.

"I love it when you get all bossy, Ms. Novak."

"Shut up and kiss me."

* * *

"Is he gone?" Lottie asked.

Aliana turned to her friend and saw her looking at her through swollen eyelids. She had been beaten while under the tender mercies of San Marcos. She had two broken ribs and a broken wrist.

"Yes, he's gone."

"You seem to have come out of your shell," she teased. Aliana glanced sharply at Lottie, unable to believe that she was making jokes at a time like this. Not because Hunter was leaving but because of Ernie. She got close to her bedside and saw the tears running down her face.

"Ah, Girlfriend, you don't have to be the life of the party for me," Aliana whispered. She touched the splint on Lottie's arm that showed up so white against her caramel colored skin. "Let me be here for you like you've always been there for me."

"There's no need," Lottie's voice was toneless.

"What do you mean?"

"I mean that it's over. I don't need any consolation, I'm so far past that point, that I'm not even going to look for any."

"It hasn't even been a day. You'll feel differently tomorrow."

Lottie's eyes met hers. "Honey, I have the piece of paper

on the wall. I know things. Here's what I know. A heart can only hold so much sorrow before it shuts down."

Aliana knew better than to try to change her mind. Time would be the only thing that could heal the pain. Even now, despite all the inroads Hunter had made, she still found it hard to believe there might be a future for the two of them. The fact that he had to go so suddenly seemed to be a harbinger of things to come. Maybe it would be for the best if—

"Stop it!" Lottie commanded from her hospital bed.

"Stop what?"

"Stop setting things up for failure before they've even started."

"Is that what your piece of paper tells you?" Aliana let the sarcasm fly. "Lucky for you, I happen to agree with you. I'm sick and tired of letting old tapes run my life. But you better watch out my friend because that also means I'm not going to put up with your happy horseshit for very long."

Aliana leaned in and carefully hugged her friend so she didn't hurt her injuries. "I love you. Of course, you get time to grieve. But in no way shape or form do you get to spout some nonsense about your heart being out of business for good. That's just not going to happen. Not on my watch."

"Back off Aliana."

"You've had my back for years, Lottie. I'm going to return the favor. I love you."

"If you do this, I will never let you give up on Hunter," Lottie threatened.

"I'm counting on that."

CHAPTER FIFTEEN

It was four o'clock. Their SKYPE call was supposed to have taken place between one and four o'clock. Please say he would still be calling. This would be her seventh chance to see him since he'd left last month, and she needed these calls like she needed air to breathe.

Aliana refused to leave the new computer that was on top of the new desk in her new apartment. That was just one more bit of information she wanted to share with Hunter, she'd taken a lease on an apartment. It was month-to-month. It was a little more money that way, but it allowed her the flexibility to easily leave when she found the right place.

She checked her internet connection for the sixty-third time and then sat back in her office chair.

"Come on, please call."

Sakra! She was getting on her own damn nerves. She closed her eyes and took a deep breath and blew it out for a count of three. She did it five more times before checking her internet connection for the sixty-fourth time.

"Get it together," she said out loud in Czech. She reached for her purse and pulled out her wallet. She rifled through it until she found what she was looking for. She unfolded the old lined piece of paper and stopped for a moment to admire Hunter's bold printing.

Dear Aliana,

This letter closes one chapter for us, but starts another. For ten years you have given me your smiles. You made me feel better about myself, and whenever I wavered, I always chose a righteous path because I wanted you to be proud of me. Your friendship saved me.

I know you're sad I'm leaving. I know you're probably even angry, but you won't show it because you're too kind. There is no way I would ever leave you behind. You are always part of my heart. Always. But I want more. I know we each have lives to live, but I want our futures to always be connected.

Alia, I know how hellish it can be in school, but you are the strongest girl I know. Please hold on. Please continue to be my friend as our next chapter starts.

Now I'll tell you a secret, I've always needed you more than you ever needed me.

-Love
Hunter Diaz

She checked the internet connection...again. Aliana wiped away a tear. She wasn't going to get to talk to Hunter today, and she'd had so much to tell him. She folded up the letter and carefully put it back into her wallet. She thought about all of her news.

Shorinda had gotten Ana Garcia a job at the nursing home, and now, the woman only needed to work one job instead of two and a half. She had been doing a great job with Aliana's mother. As a result, the last two times she had visited, *Maminka* had recognized her.

Ana was also acting like a lioness around her two children, and she made it absolutely clear to Nicolas she considered him hers. Darla's pregnancy was progressing well, and Lottie was her birth coach. It seemed to be helping both of them heal.

But the thing that she knew would tickle the hell out of Hunter was last Saturday's upset. She'd been dying to tell him about that. Hunter had been looking kind of ragged the last time they talked. He couldn't really say anything about what was going on in his world, so she worked hard to try to be entertaining, and by God, she'd struck gold with this latest event.

They'd had to postpone the book club meeting for a month, which was just as well since Aliana had so much to get done. But when they did have it, it was a doozy. They were due to discuss Fifty Shades of Gray. Everybody was gathered, except for the lady in pink. Florence showed up to the book club fifteen minutes late. This time she wasn't wearing pink, she was wearing a black trench coat and red lipstick. Her hair was no longer pink, it was blonde.

"I can't stay long," she said. "I did want to talk about the book, though. It was transformative."

Esther gave her a long considering look.

"How so?" Velma asked.

"It occurred to me that I wasn't living my life to its fullest."

Aliana's grandmother nudged her and gave her a questioning glance. "I'll explain later," Aliana said in Czech. She was just thankful she hadn't been able to find a translation of the book in Czech for Babička like she had wanted. Aliana didn't think she could have handled having those discussions.

"Are you living your life better now?" Velma asked.

"Oh yes."

The doorbell to *Mamie's* apartment rang.

"That's probably my ride. Raoul is very punctual." Florence got up from the couch and swayed across the room. That was when Aliana noticed that the woman's stockings had seams running up the back.

Florence let in a man who had to be twenty years younger. "Everyone, this is Raoul Delacroix, he and I have a lunch and dinner date."

"My dear, it's going to last much longer than that," the man said as he kissed the side of her neck. "It was lovely meeting you." He gave a wave to the crowd and escorted Florence out the door.

"She's paying for that," Esther said.

"I don't think so," *Mamie* disagreed.

"Who gives a damn. If she is, he's worth every dime," Velma said.

"I need a drink," another woman chimed in.

She had been holding onto this nugget for a week, picturing Hunter's face when she told him. Why wasn't he calling?

"Dammit, I just wanted to see him, was that too much to ask?" she yelled in Czech. She went to the closet and pulled out her yoga mat and guitar and sat down so she could calm herself in music. For just the slightest moment as she looked at her guitar pick, she thought of using it for other things, but then she gave a relieved grin as the feeling passed.

She was in the middle of her fourth song when there was a knock on the door. She looked through the peephole and all she saw were sunflowers and daisies. It couldn't be.

"Who is it?"

"Open the door, Alia."

She'd only been in the apartment for a week, so she fumbled with the lock. She kept twisting it the wrong way. Her hands were getting sweaty.

"*Cariña*, if you don't hurry, I'm just going to break down the door," Hunter laughed.

She yanked the door open and looked up into a mound of flowers. She wanted them gone. She wanted to see him.

"Easy," he said as she shoved the flowers out of her way.

There he was. He had dimples. "Hunter, thank God you're home." He swept them both inside the apartment.

"*Cariña*, this is really nice," he said as he made his way straight to the kitchen. What was he doing? She watched him dump the flowers in the sink. Then he turned back to her, and the smile changed from happy to hungry. She thanked God again.

He pulled her into his arms. Fire exploded as their lips collided. Every pent-up feeling, every unsaid word, every lost day was set free. The lush burst of passion sent her reeling, Aliana felt like she was on a merry-go-round. The world was literally spinning around her. When she realized Hunter was carrying her, she broke free of their kiss and laughed out loud.

"Having fun?"

"I'd have more if you aimed for the bedroom, and not the couch." She swung her left arm out wide like she was literally on a carnival ride and wanted to wave it in the wind as she was whisked through the air.

Happiness radiated through her yellow bedroom as Hunter laid down beside her on top of her sunflower comforter. "I'm picking up on a theme here, *mi Amor*."

"The theme is centered around you. It always has been, it just took me a decade to realize it."

He frowned. "Seriously Aliana, I don't want to rush you."

She shoved at his shoulders so that she was leaning over him. For just a moment her brain went a little fuzzy as she took in his broad shoulders in his white t-shirt and those dimples with just the right amount of scruff. When she looked into his eyes, they were dancing. Dammit, she was so busted.

She bit her lip. He picked up the end of her braid and undid the rubber band. He started to unwind her hair. "Same thing happens to me, Chaquita. I start to say something, then

I look into your blue eyes, or I see your hair, or I look at your breasts, and I have trouble remembering my own name."

"You do?" He spread her hair out so that it covered both of them.

"Oh yeah. You leave me tongue tied quite often, Ms. Novak. Now I want to make sure we're on the same page," he began.

"Now I remember what I was going to say." Aliana bit her fingernails into the resilient muscles of his chest. She was rewarded when he sucked in a deep breath of air. She felt his body go hard. She was so glad she was wearing yoga gear, it allowed for so much more tactile stimulation than jeans.

"What? What were you going to say?"

"You are not rushing me. I want this. I want you." She saw him hesitate. "Goddammit, Hunter. One girl in college had this poster that said, 'She wasn't looking for a knight, she was looking for a sword.' Dammit, I want both! And I want them now!"

He did an ab crunch while laughing and hugging her tight.

"God, I'm in love with you Aliana. I've loved you all of my life it seems, but over the last two months I have totally, ass over teakettle, fallen *in* love with you."

"Does that mean this virgin gets her sword?"

He pulled her legs apart and centered her heat above the crotch of his jeans. His brown eyes glittered with desire. "What do you think?"

She saw him consider asking her one more time. She guessed that was what made him a knight. Well, she had an idea on how to fix that. Aliana reached down and pulled off her loose over shirt and cotton sports bra in one swift move. Hunter shut his mouth, then a slow smile showed off the creases in his cheeks.

* * *

His Alia's breasts were beautiful, but by far, it was the radiance in her eyes that held him spellbound. He searched her blue eyes for any hint of hesitancy, but all he found was delight in the moment. It was finally their time.

He wrapped his arm tighter around her waist and tilted her chin up for another kiss. Something sweeter this time, something that could have been a kiss shared between teenagers on a swing set. He savored her pretty pink mouth and licked her full bottom lip until she opened up and invited him in to weave his tongue with hers.

Aliana squirmed against him, her body telling him she needed more. God knows, his body was telling him the same damn thing. But this wasn't about him, this was all about her. He moved his hand down her throat, touching a chain. He traced it downwards to where it rested between her breasts and felt the warm medallion between his fingers. Hunter lifted his mouth and looked down.

"You kept it?"

"I've never taken it off. Well, except to get a longer chain, or when the chain broke once."

"You undo me, Alia."

"You came for me when I needed you, Hunter."

She cupped his hand in both of hers and broke his grip on the medal. She then brought it up to encompass her breast. "Ah God, it feels so much better than I ever imagined." He heard the catch in her voice.

He tried to look up into her eyes, but he couldn't. Not this time, he was entranced by the silken beauty he held. He circled one delicate tip with his thumb, and she moaned as her nipple pebbled. He brought his other hand around so he could cup both breasts and continued on with the intimate caresses. She thrust herself harder into his hold, her breath sawing in and out, and she was trembling. His gaze shot to her face, her eyes were closed, and she was smiling.

"Hunter."

"I'm here, *mi Amor*. Are you ready for more?"

Her eyes opened, and they glittered with delight. "I'm ready for everything."

He threw back his head and laughed. He turned them over, so she was lying on the bed, then he got up and took off his shirt. No other woman had made him feel more desired than this moment with his Alia. He hesitated with his belt.

"Off. We can't do this with your clothes still on."

"We have time," he said as he put a knee on the bed. Aliana sat up and startled him when she stroked his cock through the front of his jeans.

"I said take the jeans off, Boy."

Shit, she was doing her Ms. Novak voice. He grinned. He took off his belt and unbuttoned his jeans.

"You don't wear underwear?"

"Well, sometimes I do. I was in a hurry to get over here." He sat down on the side of the bed and got rid of his boots and socks. He pulled out his wallet and grabbed the condoms, leaving them on the nightstand.

He watched as she swallowed. A little of her bravado had deserted her.

"Aliana, are—"

With horror, he saw her eyes well up with tears.

"Dammit, Hunter, no teasing, no talk about swords, no nothing. This is the truth, okay?"

She had her hands clenched into fists, digging into the bedspread as she leaned forward. She was glaring at him. What had he done?

"Okay, Aliana, what's the truth?"

"You're the breath I breathe. You absolutely are, Hunter. Now can I live without you? Absolutely. I can live in the dark, somewhere near hell. I've done it for years. But I don't want to. I want to live in the light with you. Reaching for my dream scares the hell out of me, but I've finally realized it's better to reach for the dream and lose it, then to have never reached for it at all." She let go of the comforter and flung her arms around him. "So, Hunter, even if this lasts just for today, I'm going to be happy because you're my everything. I love you more than you can ever imagine."

He sat there stunned. Here he was, Hunter Diaz, the boy who ate out of dumpsters, and he had a woman who said he was her dream. He had trouble focusing as tears clouded his vision. He needed to hug this woman. Kiss this woman. Love this woman.

This time when he bared her thigh, there was no shame, his Alia knew the truth, there was nothing about her that he didn't adore. But as other parts of her body came into view, his woman was shy. He wrapped her close to him, and she buried her head into his chest.

"I can't believe I'm blushing," she grumbled.

Hunter laughed.

"And now I can't believe you're laughing."

"*Cariña*, be happy I chose laughter."

"What do you mean?"

"I could be drooling. My God, you're gorgeous." Hunter slid his hand all the way from her shoulder, down the sleek line of her back to cup her ass. She arched into his caress, pushing them closer together. Her color was still high, but Hunter was pretty sure it was from excitement. He parted her leg so he could slide his in between hers. Without any coaxing, she slid her core against his thigh.

"That feels so good."

He lowered his head and took a pink nipple into his mouth, loving her gasp of pleasure as he worried the tip with his lips and tongue. He plucked the other tip with his fingers.

"Harder."

He increased his efforts, and she moaned his name.

Hunter kept his hand on her breast, and kissed his way down her torso, along the line of her tummy, until he could get to the heart of her. Aliana resisted when he tried to coax her legs apart until he started licking her scars. It seemed that knowing she had his entire acceptance, unlocked all aspects of her.

He was fascinated by the silky golden curls that barely covered her glistening, pink folds. She was exquisite. Hunter breathed in her spicy, sweet scent and covered her with his mouth. No gasp this time. No moan. She let out a wail of pleasure as he continued to torture her. He wanted this rare moment in time to be something she could treasure.

Her liquid response made it easy for him to magnify her pleasure by slowly inching one finger inside her fiery depths. She slammed her hips upwards, silently begging for more. Hunter kept going at a pace he felt she could handle until finally he redoubled his presence inside her and spread her silken channel. Sweat dotted his forehead. He thought his cock was going to pound its way through the bed and drill a hole to China. He needed to go slow.

"Hunter, I need more. Harder or slower. Faster or Softer. Something. I need something."

Glad she straightened that out. Hunter continued to curl his tongue around her clit, around and around, while his fingers sought and found that spot inside her body that made her jolt.

"Yes. Hunter, I like that. I like that a lot."

He grinned right before he sucked her engorged flesh into his mouth, and laved it over and over again with his tongue, doing it in time with the internal caresses.

Aliana, finding pleasure, was the most beautiful sound he had ever heard in his life.

* * *

Hunter was holding her in his arms. He was always holding her. He kissed her temple.

"I love you," she whispered.

"I got that."

She pushed up on her elbows. "You're really good at that."

Apprehension flashed across Hunter's face. "Hey, I didn't mean that in a bad way. That was nothing but pure compliment."

He relaxed and dimples appeared. She slid her hand down his torso to tentatively touch his penis. As soon as she did, she smiled. He felt so good, smooth heat, over strength. She curled her hand around him and stroked.

"Honey, you keep that up and we're never going to get you your sword."

"Huh?"

He pulled her hands away from his cock and grabbed a condom off the nightstand.

"Can I put it on you?"

"Maybe next time. Or sometime next week. For now, I'm taking care of it so I can take care of you."

Aliana tried to be sneaky about it, but she took a couple of calming breaths. She knew this was going to hurt. Hunter,

God love him, was not built on the small side. She rested back down on the pillows.

White teeth gleamed in the afternoon light. "*Cariña*, I have you. It's going to be fine."

"I know," she lied.

"We're not doing anything until I've had at least five kisses." His fingers trailed down from her breast to the indent at her waist, toying with the tips of her hair.

"Five kisses? I don't understand."

"You will." His head lowered, and he kissed the tip of her nose. Aliana giggle snorted. Then because that was so funny, she ended up doing it again. Hunter laughed right along with her.

"That was number one." He then swept back her hair and kissed her right behind her left ear. She felt it in every part of her body. As he moved, he accidentally blew warm air into her ear. She shivered.

"That was number two." Hunter slid his hand down the length of her arm and entwined their fingers. He brought her hand to his mouth and brushed the softest kiss to the back of her knuckles, just like a Knight of Olde. "That's three."

He looked deep into her eyes, and then melded their lips together, in a sublime moment where the world fell away. Finally, he pulled away. "That's four."

He pushed downward, parted her legs, and found her patchwork quilt of cuts, kissing along every slice. Aliana didn't even realize she was crying until she tasted her tears. "That's five," he whispered.

"Be part of me," she begged.

"I already am, *mi Amor*, I already am," he said as he pushed his cock slowly inside of her.

If there was pain, she never realized it. How could so much heat and power be so gentle? She wrapped her arms and legs around Hunter as she tilted her body upwards to meet his tender thrusts.

"Are you okay?"

"You have to ask?"

She looked into his warm brown eyes and saw his love and concern. Her body melted even more. Drawing him in even deeper.

He kissed her, and she felt her world shift.

They moved as one. Their eyes open, they fell into one another's arms, hearts and souls. Aliana had been to hell, and now, she had found heaven in the arms of a knight. They soared into bliss together.

THE END

BIOGRAPHY

Caitlyn O'Leary is an avid reader and considers herself a fan first and an author second. She reads a wide variety of genres, but finds herself going back to happily-ever-afters. Getting a chance to write, after years in corporate America is a dream come true. She hopes her stories provide the kind of entertainment and escape she has found from some of her favorite authors.

Keep up with Caitlyn O'Leary:

Facebook: tinyurl.com/nuhvey2
Twitter: @CaitlynOLearyNA
Pinterest: tinyurl.com/q36uohc
Goodreads: tinyurl.com/nqy66h7
Website: www.caitlynoleary.com
Email: caitlyn@caitlynoleary.com
Newsletter: http://bit.ly/1WIhRup
Instagram: http://bit.ly/29WaNIh

BOOKS BY CAITLYN O'LEARY

The Found Series
Revealed, Book One
Forsaken, Book Two
Healed, Book Three

Midnight Delta Series
Her Vigilant SEAL, Book One
Her Loyal SEAL, Book Two
Her Adoring SEAL, Book Three
Sealed with a Kiss, A Midnight Delta Novella, Book Four
Her Daring SEAL, Book Five
Her Fierce SEAL, Book Six
Protecting Hope, Book Seven (*Seal of Protection &
Midnight Delta Crossover Novel; Susan Stoker KindleWorld*)
A SEAL's Vigilant Heart, Book Eight
Her Dominant SEAL, Book Nine
Her Relentless SEAL, Book Ten
Her Treasured SEAL, Book Eleven

Black Dawn Series
Her Steadfast Hero, Book One
Her Devoted Hero, Book Two
Her Passionate Hero, Book Three

Shadow Alliance
Declan, Book One
Cooper's Promise, Companion Novel
(*Omega Team and Shadow Alliance
Crossover Novel; Desiree Holt KindleWorld*)

The Sisters Series
Tempting Fire, Book One (*Sisters Series and Dallas Fire & Rescue Crossover Novel; Paige Tyler KindleWorld*)

Fate Harbor Series Published by Siren/Bookstrand
Trusting Chance, Book One
Protecting Olivia, Book Two
Claiming Kara, Book Three
Isabella's Submission, Book Four
Cherishing Brianna, Book Five